I0886040

THE EMPLOYEE

THE EMPLOYEE

Jacques Sternberg

translated by Matt Seidel

WAKEFIELD PRESS / CAMBRIDGE, MASSACHUSETTS

This translation © 2025 Wakefield Press

Wakefield Press, P.O. Box 425645, Cambridge, MA 02142
Originally published as *L'employé* in 1958.
Original French text © 2021 by Éditions de Minuit
Frontispiece: Handmade collage by Allan Kausch

All rights reserved. No part of this book may be reproduced in any form by any electronic or mechanical means (including photocopying, recording, or information storage and retrieval) without permission in writing from the publisher.

This book was set in Garamond Premier Pro and Helvetica Neue Pro by Wakefield Press. Printed and bound by Versa Press in the United States of America.

ISBN: 978-1-962728-05-8

Available through D.A.P./Distributed Art Publishers
75 Broad Street, Suite 630
New York, New York 10004
Tel: (212) 627-1999
Fax: (212) 627-9484

1 2 3 4 5 6 7 8 9 10

TRANSLATOR'S INTRODUCTION

I

Jacques Sternberg's *The Employee*, originally published by Les Éditions de Minuit in 1958, is in one sense a novel about different forms of productivity. A nameless employee stands outside the door to his office, hesitating to enter because he is five minutes late. Between then and the last page, when he opens the door one minute later, he embarks on an epic daydreaming session whose quicksilver, often bewildering episodes make up the entire novel. A solid day's work, narratively at least. When he enters the office, his boss rebukes him for his repeated, and potentially job-ending, tardiness: "What goes through that head of yours . . ." If he only knew . . . The employee's fertile (and terrifying) imagination represent a threat best kept out of the workplace.

The novel's narrator is not necessarily lazy, unmotivated, unthinking, or unproductive but, rather, hard at work in his daydreams. In these visions, he churns out correspondence, pounds the pavement, makes sales calls, starts a mining operation, works for a shadowy sewer civil service organization, and directs a film, though he does admittedly also carve out time for various erotic and interstellar adventures. Yet even these are filtered through his identity as an employee. His business entanglements follow him to the outer reaches of the universe, and his desire for unattainable, unworldly, or spectral women dictates his professional path(s). So committed is he to tracking down one woman after a brief interaction that he takes a job at the local gas company (alas, she uses coal), then as a tax inspector (she is a dodger), then as a private detective (*cherchez la femme*!), then as a mathematician (to discover the "square root of her charm"), and finally as a coroner (successfully so, sadly). Here the metamorphosing employee demonstrates Sternberg's aptitude for reversing received ideas: he seeks not a purpose in his profession but instead a profession to fulfill his purpose.

Sternberg estimated that he traveled roughly 350,000 kilometers over the course of his life on his preferred vehicle, a Solex scooter, which topped out at what he considered an ideal speed: 35 kilometers per hour. That tame velocity might be surprising, given the rapid-fire succession of scene shifts and metamorphoses that characterize *The Employee* and indeed Sternberg's career as a whole.

In the preface to the pocket edition of one of Sternberg's most successful commercial novels, *Toi, ma nuit* (1965)—an erotic dystopian fiction Sternberg claims anticipated the sexual revolution by several years—the French publisher Éric Losfeld summed up the eclectic writer of absurdist tales, science fiction, erotica, and black humor:

> It must be said that Sternberg likes neither labels nor flags; he won't let himself be confined to any one genre. He was described as a virtuoso of brevity, then took it upon himself to write interminable novels. He was seen as the best hope for French science fiction, then hastened to abandon the genre and shout from the rooftops that he hated it; he was pegged as a humorist and awarded the Black Humor Prize in 1961 for his lone poignant novel.[1]

That novel was *The Employee*, which has enjoyed a special place among Sternberg's vast oeuvre of nearly fifty works put out by many French major publishing houses. (In the same preface, Losfeld calls Sternberg a "serial breaker of contracts.") "Poignant" is not the first word that comes to mind when reading the novel, though there is some degree of pathos in the hapless narrator's journey through space and time. Spun round and round on the Wheel of Fortune, he strives, and more often than not fails, to master the bizarre logic governing his ever-shifting environment. Moreover, one gets the sense that no matter the degradations the employee has endured in his imaginary flight, what reality has in store for him might be worse.

Like the workday, this novel can be an exercise in endurance. Stationary though the narrator might be, his account gallops across genres and modes and galaxies. His protean character is defined through his myriad evolutions. Every expression provides an opportunity for wordplay and every scenario chugs inexorably toward strange, grotesque, and entropic derailments, after which the game narrator resets to be thrust into a new journey. Later in his career, Sternberg would abandon the novel and exclusively write stories—droll, fantastical, satirical, and very short. (Incidentally, he was proud that two of his books boasted the longest tables of contents in French literature: the science-fiction-tinged tales of *Contes glacés* [270 entries] and the absurdist fare of *188 Contes à régler*.) *The Employee*, by contrast, is an exhaustive work in which a man responds to the threat of a seemingly endless workday with his limitless fancy.

II

Jacques Sternberg was born in Anvers, Belgium, as Nathan Sternbaum, the son of a Jewish diamond cutter. A hopeless student, he found refuge from the abuse of his stern Flemish teachers in bicycling and American cinema, including the comedies of Laurel and Hardy. Sternberg was as fond of literary criticism as he was of psychoanalysis, but he did appreciate Hélène

Oswald's evaluation of him as a "galactic idiot" whose educational shortcomings gave his imagination free rein: "In essence, your originality stems entirely from the fact that you've always been a dunce."[2] Stay out of school, kids.

In 1938, as World War II approached, Sternberg's family fled Belgium to France's Côte d'Azur, where they stayed for four years before fleeing once more, crossing the Pyrenees into Spain. The family was arrested and detained in Barcelona before being returned to France and the Camp de Gurs, from which the majority of Jews were sent to Drancy, and then to gas chambers. (His father would die in transport to a Polish camp.) In a miraculous stroke of luck, a Gur camp official was struck by his youth and vitality and destroyed his file. There was no longer any record of him: he had no name, nationality, "was neither Jew nor Aryan," as he put in his memoir *Profession: Mortel: fragments d'autobiographie*. After escaping during a transfer, Sternberg, under the name Claude Sabatier, eventually made his way to Paris, returning to his native Belgium in 1944 in an American Army jeep.

Back in Belgium, he would read several of his short fantastical stories each week at a club called "La Poubelle," and worked for a time as a packager. When he and his wife, Francine, decided to move to Paris several years later, his employer quipped, "We are losing a bad writer, but a great packager."[3] Taste is subjective, of course, but the employer was arguably wrong on not one but two counts: The packing phenom once sliced off the tip of his thumb on the job. (Toward the end of *The Employee*, the narrator encounters his automaton-like double working at a mall and zealously wrapping everything, from parcels to people, he can get his nimble, chaotically productive hands on: a surreal example of Henri Bergson's classic definition of comedy, "something mechanical encrusted upon the living."[4])

During Sternberg's first years living in Paris, he supported his wife and young son working as a typist, sales rep, and agent for a book of the month club. He wrote on the clock as much as possible, churning out short stories and novels that, as he recounted with a tinge of pride, would be refused by the entire Parisian literary establishment. In 1953, however, Losfeld came across a copy of the story collection *La géometrie de l'impossible*, which Sternberg had handprinted, and published them at his press, Le Terrain Vague. Next came a Dostoyevskyan novel of alienation and crime called *Le Délit* (1954) and a science fiction novel, *La sortie est au fond de l'espace* (1956), in which humanity must take to space after a microbe runs havoc over the Earth.

In the late 1950s and 1960s, Sternberg attained a measure of financial security through overseeing the humor pages of *Arts* magazine, writing a column for *Magazine Littéraire*, and assembling anthologies drawn from *Planète*, Jacques Bergier and Louis Pauwels's influential magazine of "fantastic realism." After reading *Toi, ma nuit*, the New Wave director Alain Resnais engaged Sternberg to write a screenplay, *Je t'aime, je t'aime* (1968), about a machine that allows a man to revisit moments from a past relationship. Sternberg blamed the film's poor initial reception on the 1968 protests that prematurely shut down the International Film Festival in Cannes, where it was to be screened. He was also involved with the short-lived Panic Movement, an outgrowth of surrealism started by Fernando Arrabal, Alejandro Jodorowsky, and Roland Topor, whose wonderfully macabre illustrations grace many of Sternberg's texts.

Sternberg was a skeptical, antinomian fixture of the Parisian literary scene for decades. In a wry section of his memoir entitled "Contacts," he mocks the incredible nature of autobiographical anecdotes ("Almost everyone has hunted rhinos with Hemingway, screwed Ava Gardner, and had an orgy with the Queen of Sheba")[5] before inventorying the authors and celebrities with whom he had modest encounters: Samuel Beckett walking past him in the hallway of Les Éditions de Minuit; Marguerite Yourcenar making awkward conversation at a luncheon; Jacques Prévert showing him his collages; cheering alongside Claude Chabrol at a French Open tennis match; and receiving a flirtatious smile from Brigitte Bardot. One senses from such passages how he was both inside and outside the establishment, a prolific author who could always find a publisher if not, to his chagrin, a large audience. He is refreshingly honest that despite his reputation as an iconoclast, "un écrivain maudit" as Losfeld called him, nothing would have meant more to him than being published by Éditions Gallimard, the most prestigious of French houses. (He would have to settle for appearing under the house's pocket imprint, Folio, twice.)

III

Sternberg dreamed of writing a taut, glacial novel, a chiseled short work of under 200 pages in the mode of Walter Tevis's *The Hustler* or Georges Simenon's *The Widow*. By his own admission, he never produced such a work, though with *The Employee*, Jérôme Lindon, Minuit's publisher, did his part by cutting down the original 350-page manuscript by nearly half to a more manageable dose of delirium. Sternberg's writerly energies were more anarchic, fluid. Sternberg wrote that for a novel to captivate him, all that was needed was one character "adrift among his everyday muddle or fantasies."[6] *The Employee* certainly captivates under this rubric. From the very first lines, in which the tardy narrator abruptly launches into his unconventional upbringing, he, along with readers, is set adrift within Sternberg's oceanic imagination. Sternberg identified heavily with the sea and spent untold hours navigating it in his prized Sunfish boat, a sleek dinghy in which he could indulge his "visceral need to drift along in a pleasant waste of time, my aptitude to merely spin around without wanting to get anywhere."[7]

The employee's tale is full of abrupt temporal and spatial jumps—with frequent shifts from present to past tense—but follows a general biographical trajectory. He recounts his feral childhood with hundreds of siblings and a band of savage fathers. His mother is a "famous nymphomaniac" who eventually finds an outlet for her spiritual and corporal passions by becoming a prostitute in a Benedictine monastery. Left on his own, the boy heads out into the world that seems to have been constructed through some collaboration between Ovid and Lewis Carroll. (Beckett and Ionesco are more contemporary influences, Sternberg having been mesmerized by a sparsely attended performance of the latter's *Les Chaises* in 1952.) Landscapes and bodies mutate in surreal dreamscapes governed by absurdist logic. Normal developmental paths—biological, professional—are reversed. In one episode, he devolves into a larval state, in another, he works his way *down* the corporate ladder, much to his delight. Interrogated by the police on suspicion of murder—he lives, like a Kafka character, under a near-constant presumption of guilt—the narrator is damned by the *lack* of evidence against him:

> "You're wondering how we managed to find the body, right?" the inspector said. "As it happens, we haven't found it. That's precisely what points to you. Let's consider it logically: if you hadn't killed her, you'd have had no reason to hide the body, and we would have found it. Therefore, since we did not find it, you must have killed her. Crystal clear, no?"

In absurdist works, the fictional universe tends to be both liberating—from the laws of physics, morality, sense—and confining. Wonderland is all fun and games until Alice runs afoul of the rules, no less serious for being nonsensical. *The Employee* consistently plays with this tension. On the one hand, the employee is "malleable, extremely subject to change," and the physical and temporal barriers around him are always collapsing, washed away by floods or tempests. On the other, he is always in danger of becoming fixed in time or space: trapped within the sap of cherry tree; tethered to a grindstone for an office blunder; confined within a year of Sundays; languishing between 9:00 and 9:15 a.m. as years pass and colleagues advance in their careers; stuck within a film of his own devising; or marooned within the hellscape of a retail mall. There is a play between the expansive and contractive natures of the protagonist's universe, one that mirrors the novel's central tension: the narrator's unbounded imagination as he hesitates just outside the office door and the restrictive employment waiting for him on the other side.

Another point of fixity is his wife Mygale, whom one could describe as long-suffering if she evinced any emotion whatsoever. The narrator periodically finds himself back in the family apartment, usually in some newly degraded state, where Mygale and their young son greet his arrival with indifference. Yet the taciturn, stoic woman is also the novel's center of gravity, both literal and figurative: a port in the storm and welcome narrative dead end for the story-tossed protagonist.

Sternberg said that he wrote *The Employee* in a "vertiginous" state of inspiration. He had the impression of being dictated to for several months before producing, "almost unbeknownst to me," the "torrential" text.[8] The narrator himself is besieged by external voices—mysterious, seductive, peremptory, insistent—that resonate throughout the novel. These voices are as likely to seduce as to hector him, or both, as in the novel's most spectacular scene set in a shopping mall that rises up in an impenetrable jungle. That section's narrator is a loudspeaker, whose "honeyed voice, servile and dictatorial," conveys the sirenic bombardment of capitalism as it urges all-too-willing customers to participate in the highest bill contest, assures shoppers that in the event they are fatally poisoned by a product the store will furnish a replacement and cover funeral costs, and helpfully informs visitors that the mall exit is free with any purchase over 3,000 francs.

Spaced over three chapters, the mall episode demonstrates Sternberg at his best. What could have been a targeted lampooning of consumerist culture becomes a more encyclopedic, or in this context inflationary, satirical vision, sublime in its scope and strangeness. It's been over sixty years since the publication of this oddity from a sui generis writer—high time for an English translation. As the tardy protagonist, if not his employer, might concur: Better late than never.

NOTES

1. Éric Losfeld, "Preface," *Toi, Ma Nuit*, by Jacques Sternberg (Paris: 10/18, 1974), translation mine.
2. Jacques Sternberg, *Profession: Mortel: fragments d'autobiographie* (Paris: Societe d'édition Les Belles Lettres, 2001), 209–10, translation mine.
3. Sternberg, *Profession: Mortel*, 87.
4. Henri Bergson, "Laughter," in *Comedy*, ed. Wylie Sypher (Baltimore: The Johns Hopkins University Press, 1980), 84.
5. Sternberg, *Profession: Mortel*, 56.
6. Sternberg, *Profession: Mortel*, 191.
7. Sternberg, *Profession: Mortel*, 267.
8. Sternberg, *Profession: Mortel*, 241.

THE EMPLOYEE

STANDING AT THE DOOR, I checked the time: five past ten. I hesitated a moment.

I was lucky to have been born to well-off but triviparous parents. My mother was a famous nymphomaniac: she lent her name to an anthology of vice that remains authoritative. Her gaze boiled up like incandescent lava from her rheumy eyes, and her body was one giant tentacle devoured by its own voracity. My brothers and sisters—we numbered more than four hundred—lived with us on the city outskirts in a vast, red-brick apartment block reserved for our exclusive use. Occasionally a nasty flu would knock off several dozen of our clan, but no one noticed: in one night, my mother easily managed to double the losses from any epidemic. The fathers, whom it would be difficult to count, claimed the lower floors, and an endless chamber music of their reproachful screams and my mother's wheezing would blare out through the walls of that fortress.

I probably don't need to mention the dilapidated conditions in which this community lived. No one ever thought of cleaning up the countless unfurnished rooms we inhabited, dressed in rags and in a state of absolute filth. We fed primarily on the meat our mother tossed us in passing and the provisions suppliers brought along in her wake.

Around the age of thirty, however, my mother abandoned this dissipated life and took refuge in a portside brothel, where she still leads the saintly existence of a Benedictine prostitute, spending her easygoing days in prayer, spasms, and bookkeeping.

Her departure led to some disturbances. Because it was the rainy season and the fathers were a generally unpleasant lot, they rubbed each other out one by one. The children, now a savage horde of orphans, grew up in absolute chaos. Debilitated by alcohol and abuse, most died at a young age. Twenty-five perished in a memorable game of hunt-the-thimble; some killed themselves. The survivors created a death lottery that distributed numerous prizes. But if each day saw a new corpse, each night brought a birth, as we all slept together, on top of one another, and many of our sisters shared their mother's famous ardor.

One night, though, a group of fathers organized a punitive raid to avenge one of their own, whom we had put to death for a laugh. They attacked the building with grenades and quickly leveled it. I escaped the massacre by chance: that night, I had been strung up by my feet from the highest point on the roof in an effort to avoid wetting my bed.

Now an orphan, I was taken in by a music-loving uncle, who made me into his own personal organ. Unfortunately, this philanthropist was so pious that he eventually had to be abandoned in an empty field, where he proved useful in mending an old fence. Left on my own, I decided to enter an organage.

I rang the doorbell. The establishment instantly transformed into a bathroom. The lead ceiling was low, menacing. The ocean came right up to its high walls, sharks jumping out of the soapy water and occasionally ramming into the partitions. At night, we would find them in the gutters, where the rooftop bums carved them up.

I entered the water after consulting a map of the surroundings, which indicated that I should be just left of the Philippines. I let myself float down to the bottom of this abyss. When I came to a stop after five hours of diving, I was in a field. It was cold, but beautiful; the air was dry. Had I returned to Europe along the bottom of the ocean? It seemed a safe assumption, since a Michelin road marker told me that I was two kilometers from Auxerre.

I was completely unfamiliar with the region and got lost in thirty seconds. The first time it happened, I had the good fortune to find myself on a street corner. The second time, in the window of an antique shop. It took me a week to buy myself back, after quite a few sacrifices. Not to mention the effort I put in: it was tough working with just my feet, as I couldn't buy back either my hands or my misconceptions, which were unaffordable. But it was becoming clear with each new purchase that I would soon be a true collector. I scooped up some pairs of hands for my old age; I stashed some used replacement eyes in my cupboard. I even managed to find a reversible face and a beach torso that came with a toolkit. I enjoyed the satisfaction of knowing that I was a self-made man.

Then came the typhoid monsoon that ruined everything.

The monsoon brought a kind of amorphous hail, which abruptly transformed into a jolt of silence; this silence provided lobstras just about everywhere, which we believed were edible and which turned out to be more anostress than any bordalouse. Conditions would have certainly improved had a terrible cybergale not swept up everything in its path the next day, injecting the seeds of a deadly trysele into all the flyges. A deluge of mirtacles fell in slow motion, and when they finally mixed in with the rain, the morrible sargase that would terrorize the whole world exploded in a single flash of maurse.

Everything was about to start over.

EVERYTHING STARTED OVER.

Of a delicate constitution since birth, my body was fortified by the bad weather and soon developed in a satisfactory manner.

I was only seven when my third arm emerged. Then came my second head, but it lacked a jaw, a little particularity that cast a shadow over my family's happiness. And that very same night, one of my four eyes got lost in some recess of my skull. We looked for it for a long time, in vain.

When I was around eight, small hands grew from the ends of each of my fingers; then other hands from the fingers of those little hands. They were decorative but not very practical, which partly explains why I couldn't find a real job before the age of nine. At that point, my hands in effect withered and fell like dead leaves. They were replaced by transparent scales that covered my entire body. One night, one of them bit me, and I tore them all out in a rage.

When my head finally fell off, I reached the age of reason.

Then came the molting. As I lost my feathers, I, who was born deaf and blind, recovered my speech and grew up a paralytic.

I enjoyed unfailing good health. When I sneezed, I shattered every window in the neighborhood, but I only had to breathe for them to repair themselves. I wasn't very big, except in the morning, between ten and eleven, when I easily surpassed four meters.

Everything did me good: a meager slice of bread fattened me up; a glass of water got me drunk; a walk in the fresh air gave me six or seven extra legs. And after each erotic dream, every woman in the neighborhood found herself pregnant.

I was malleable, extremely subject to change. At night, I mimetically grew as dark as the shadow of a shadow. When in water, I became a deep-sea fish, slithering, oviparous, and, if need be, invisible when encountering the slightest danger. Lighter than air when I wished to be, I floated straight up without even realizing it. I changed from one color to another just by flipping through a paint sample catalog. When I extended a hand to a friend, it would inevitably be replaced by a robotic one. A battery-less source of energy, I could stand in for any turbine, and to save on the electricity bill, my mother often hooked me up to her sewing machine or electric razor. One could read the precise time on my face, aromatic herbs grew between my hairs, and my nails were a source of ivory. A very expensive elixir was distilled from my tears, my words could be transmuted into silver ingots, my silence into fine gold, and my sweat gave our daily bread a smoky flavor. I provided hot water in the morning; at noon, the household gas; at night, I served as the television. A little of my blood mixed with snow produced an unctuous foam that could be incorporated into various sauces or made into soap powder. Water evaporated when I dipped my finger in it, and I picked up soundwaves as well as radiation, transforming them into colors; I emitted long-distance ultraviolet rays and translated messages from space into free verse as I slept.

Every object suggested a new idea to me, and from each new idea emerged a new object. I had only to turn on the faucet to reformulate hydrostatic laws, hear one syllable to reconstruct the entire network of significations it could suggest, hear one clean tone to spin out any symphony whatsoever. Even when I thought of nothing, I ended up accomplishing something, and were I to contemplate nothingness, I doubtless would have rapidly transformed it into a closed and climatized system. From a branch, I fashioned a radio tower; from a wheel, a supersonic car; from a slice of ham, one or two pigs in perfect health. I reinvented the world even while sleeping, waking up amid a heap of equations. Hiding pencils and paper would have done nothing; it was so easy to conjure up more in my sleep.

These innocent games concluded when I lost my two wings. Gaunt, weakened, I changed from the butterfly I once was into a larva, then a cocoon. For the most part, I was left out in the garden, where I would target the trees. It was a cherry tree that snagged me in its sap and swallowed me.

For several years I was this tree, which one month turned into a poplar. It was even claimed that it produced oranges one year, then orangeades. But I think things got exaggerated. I remember very little from this time: most trees don't think much. I could have lived like that, larval and unconscious, for centuries, had my father not gotten the idea to buy a small war secondhand, which he unleashed in our garden. A mortar shell struck down the tree that had swallowed me. Thus did my parents rediscover me, fully grown but healthy and safe.

So great was their disappointment that it brought on a flood. After the waters had receded, they were delighted to see that their modest house, which along with the garden had been washed away by the water, had landed on the roof of a palace of marble and calcium, half stuck in the marsh of a vast park whose owners had drowned. My father, who had remained a simple man, devoted himself to acting as beadle to this residence, which he strove to set up as a suburban cathedral. He spent his days halberd at the ready and tipped himself every Saturday night, albeit with relative modesty, as he was born stingy. One Sunday, when he had come back dead-drunk from mass, he fired himself immediately, and we never saw him again.

My mother was now on her own and wandered for a long time through the dwelling's 280 rooms and ended up getting lost. We sent two explorers to track her down, but one died of thirst in the grand salon and the other disappeared on a shifting parquet floor. So I went to file a claim for her at the office of lost parents. They granted me a small indemnity and a backup mother to hold me over. She had my mother's attributes, if not her charm. I can still picture her on winter nights, neck deep in laundry, when she'd set her beautiful head on the mantle and her little worker's hands scurried from one corner of the rug to another, while our pet fish came to warm themselves before the open fire. I remember her begging our neighbor for some water and then cooking it, which constituted our only meal during hard times. She broke down the remaining water from these dinners herself to hastily concoct the air we needed but couldn't afford to buy in tubes. Then, from the dried and smoked water, she would derive a very nourishing dish we would eat on holidays. So destitute were we that she would have to go into town to sell whatever milligrams of tungsten she managed to extract from our annual consumption of liquid.

This went on until the day she was called up to the army reserves. She returned from the barracks transformed, almost jingoistic, and, attracted to his uniform, married a ticket inspector at the Mèvres-Rabylone station,[1] who, one year later on the quai de Senfert-Mochereau, punched her ticket for good in a fit of rage. She apparently died content, relieved to note that her horoscope, which had predicted that the end of her days would be terribly distressing, proved for once to be accurate.

YEARS PASSED. One after the other when December thirty-firsts stored memories of the year's events, one into the other when, for some reason, clocks stopped ticking. Some of them went by very slowly and were more acrid than a cloud of toxic gas; others, by contrast, sped by like lightning, ungraspable, like those large phosphorescent fish that swim in the sky on very dark nights.

Little incidents sometimes livened things up: the Earth stopped turning for a moment, quivered with fear before some hostile alien, and closed over its parasitic inhabitants. But no one noticed that in year 38, for the entire month of January, the world operated outside the laws of gravity. Nor did anyone notice that the year 45 had been removed from the calendar: not a single complaint on the matter.

That whole year, I was dogged by bad luck.

I lost my job one Monday in the subway. Then again, I did find one of my favorite brothers drowned in the aquarium of one of the most fashionable downtown cafés. And that same day, the distress message in a bottle that I had launched across the capital didn't lead to the happy ending I had envisioned. The bottle injured a passerby, who had me arrested. When I got out of prison, I discovered that my apartment had been invaded by treasure hunters who, hoping to find gold, were tearing up the floors, walls, and ceilings. As for my wife, won over by faith, she had taken the veil, embarked on the high seas, and, with the wind at her back, sailed around the world, leaving behind all its charms.

For months nothing went my way, not even lucky breaks. Culinary explosions followed fast upon tornadoes targeting me alone, such that any brief respite ultimately seemed to signal a coming misfortune. A banal reflection addressed to a wall could land me in big trouble, as if everything around me was nothing but a gigantic mirror eager to seize the many aspects of my culpability. The flowers on my wallpaper withered when I looked at them, the ground under my feet grew swampy when the temperature rose above 10 degrees Celsius, and my household tools could become animate and claw into me, leaving me with oozing burns that constantly bothered me. I brought bad luck to everyone I encountered; I delivered catastrophe to their doorstep. A mere letter from me was generally equivalent to a death warrant; hands that I touched had to be amputated immediately to avoid gangrene; my reflection shattered store windows, and when I closed a door behind me, I often caused the whole building to disappear. Tossing away an extinguished match usually started a fire across the whole neighborhood.

Luck continued to prove elusive even during the war.

Working as a spy, I zealously served the enemy's ambassador, who had taken me on as a valet; he furnished me with excellent references, which I could accept unabashedly, knowing that I had never swiped any document nor even a piece of silver from him. My own side had no choice but to recall me back to the infantry. My very presence there provoked us into making two strategic retreats and led to one idiotic debacle as well as a spectacular defeat, immortalized by the thousands of painters who, brushes in hand, stormed onto the glorious field of battle. When, in a solo attack wielding a bayonet against cannons, I finally went on the offensive, assaulting a farmstead, then two trenches, and then arriving as a conqueror storming the enemy's capital city, which I wished to occupy after proclaiming martial law, I was politely informed that the war had ended two months earlier. It hadn't done me much good.

Defeated, but forever seeking an object of desire, I had no choice but to forge on. How many thousands of women did I approach that year? In vain, alas. Mere encounters, names, faces, or bodies without a face . . . Tierce, Alcède, Myrne, Diurne, Colcide, Adragase, Argoule, what's become of you? In fact, have you just now come into being? You barely existed when first I met you.

Diurne, who like a mirage only appeared when it was extremely hot. Colcide, who one morning lost the right side of her face that I so adored. Erguèle, whom I followed silently for three days and nights, accompanying her to the office, trailing her to restaurants, strolling all day by her side, pursuing her in her dreams. Démisure, hidden within her marvelous platinum blonde hair that was like a jungle of dried seaweed. Démisure, whom I lusted after in vain for one whole night without ever managing to reach the body burrowed in that nest.

So many names, yes. Ylge, Orguèle, Mornose, Sylcyde, Aliace, these and others, leaving aside those whose names I never asked, nor those who passed by me on the sidewalk and whom I never had the courage to approach . . . Did they really exist? Were they more real than the women who never crossed my path? What does it even matter, since I never found the name of the one woman to whom I could devote myself? Because that's how it is: first and foremost, there was Y. Who will always remain unknown to me.

I had noticed her one morning in an office and said just a few words to her. She replied with a yes, then a no. This unforgettable dialogue remains my sole memory of her. All told, I had barely even looked at her, but I could still call up her face two days later. No point in denying it: I treasured her, treasured only her, had never treasured anyone but her, thought of nothing else but seeing her, touching her, speaking to her. I immediately returned to her office, but she no longer worked there. Nobody knew her name or address, nor where she came from. How to convey all my efforts to find her? I thought of nothing else for weeks, flipping through the phone book from front to back to see if her face would happen to materialize before a name. She probably didn't have a telephone. Careless of the cost, I took a census of every gray-eyed woman, though by then her eyes could have turned green. I got a job at a gas company to locate her, then as a tax inspector, then as a detective, all for naught. I had to conclude that she used coal for heat, that she didn't pay taxes, that she had no private life to speak of. I called out to her over the airwaves and television screens. I studied mathematics and algebra to discover the syllables of her name by calculating the square root of her charm. No luck.

I did, however, find her one year later when, having almost given up hope, I took a job at the morgue. I instantly recognized her when I opened the refrigerated drawer and saw her face; death, it must be admitted, became her. When I looked over her death certificate, I saw that her identity was listed as "Unknown."

What to say about Istrigale, with whom I could do whatever I wished because she had managed to bridge the gulf separating the real from the unimaginable? I occasionally watched her enter a crystalline non-world from which she would return, alluring as ever. More than once, I buried her in a mud pit so that I would have the pleasure of unearthing her with a pickaxe amid dazzling crystallizations of precious stones. I made her as fluid as cloudy water, as dense as mercury, as transparent as ice, as terrifying as a ghost with razor blades for hair, and yet also smiling, eager to offer me her desire. I conferred upon her a licentiousness to match her plunging neckline. Her eyes smoldered, her hands were webbed, and her face was upside-down. I transfused into her every sort of chemical mixture with the most contradictory passions. I projected her across centuries of the eternal feminine and injunctions to "never beat a woman with a rose," and each time she came back to me with that ironic and glacial look that neither terror nor passion ever managed to render unambiguous. One day, she nicked her finger while cutting a piece of bread, and though barely bleeding, died within ten seconds, exsanguinated.

Then came Druse, whom I lost just as suddenly, just as brutally. Druse, whom I called Polaris, was not only frigid but perpetually iced over. She would invite me over, as it happens, to the large butcher's refrigerator in which she lived.

How to describe Chlirode? Chilrode, whom I found more charming than the others. I was to meet up with her as planned on a Thursday, but that month Wednesdays had assumed such importance that it was decreed that Thursdays would be eliminated for the benefit of Fridays, which counted double with the slowdown resulting from the compressed Montuesdays.

There was also Fyctige, who, like a bat, was nocturnal and would return to my place through the window. For months, she was mine without my ever seeing her face. Then, little by little, panic took hold of me. I started thinking that I was sleeping with a monster, a woman with the face of a medusa or a large, shapeless hole. Rattled, I left her.

That's how I came to know Galène. I had met her on vacation when I was visiting the planet Tryge, 63 million kilometers from the Grand Chasms Galaxy. I brought her back to Earth and married her. But once back on Earth, she grew younger and younger every day. I left her, regretfully, when she had reached the age of twelve. To get her out of my mind, I traveled even farther afield. In order to see Aldrèse, whom I had met in a dream, I became the first man to push beyond the Purple Line. I searched for her on the planet Ictus, but once over there I realized that I had confused that land with Ictos, which was in a galaxy much farther away, and inaccessible to boot, as it was deep within the domain of the giant space medusas. When I finally returned to Earth, I was informed that Aldrèse had come to my place, waited there a long time, but died of boredom a week before I got back.

I met Ybillia. I never once saw her without her knitting needles. It was her sole passion, her only concern. It took me weeks to convince her to drop her needlework for a few minutes. I led her to the bed, undressed her. In her hair, I noticed a little string of wool between two braids. I pulled on it. I pulled on it for two hours. When I came to the end, I had a gigantic ball of wool in my hands, but I had undone Ybilla.

I really couldn't catch a break that year.

Things looked to be improving in November, though, when I discovered that gold mine in a public garden in the center of town. Extracting it wasn't easy, as I had to work quickly during the cheaper low-usage hours between two and four in the morning. But I was rewarded for my efforts by the fortune I dug up from those well-combed grounds. Still, I couldn't shake my bad luck: one morning, I was given my gas bill for the previous three months. It came to some six million-odd francs. That same day, my only backer caught the financial plague and died spitting up gold. The following day, I noticed that a thirty-floor apartment building had sprung up overnight on the park grounds.

Demoralized, I decided to give up. They buried me on a fall morning under a driving rain. I died two days later. From a bad cold. I never could tolerate humidity.

WHAT DO YOU DO once you're dead?

Lament your state? Resuscitate yourself? But that would be so exhausting. Better to hover between life and death in a state of inertia. That simplifies everything. You just have to stay put with your eyes open and disembark wherever you wish—on the morning of 8 November, for example.

It had been a sinister night. One of those seemingly anodyne evenings destined to unspool in a comforting apartment whose nondescript decor becomes unrecognizable when two in the morning rolls around.

And I did in fact wake with a start at two in the morning. Panicked upon sensing that nothing had happened, that nothing would ever happen. Yet I had heard the whole apartment slowly moving forward during the night, groping its way along, creaking like a new shoe. Or rather, it was simply that nocturnal entity which strolled through the rooms grazing on the floor, the walls, feeding on the colors. I got up to hunt it, but how was I to capture it? I could barely feel it twitching between the chair cushions, under the floorboards, or moving from one book to another in the library. More worrisome to me at that moment was the shriek of the cat. It was no longer a meowing, but the shadow of a meowing. A silent scream, like a wheeze. I had opened the bathroom door and seen a translucent, limp creature in the night, an X-ray of a cat. Otherwise, it looked perfectly fine. Smiling from ear to ear, from claw to claw, it huffed upon spotting me.

The floor became a sludgy marsh whose tall flowers of mud slowly dripped along the walls. Listening closely, one could already detect the lapping of a sort of animate slime, perhaps nothing more than the vital organ of some house octopus. Before heading back to my bedroom, I opened a door I hadn't noticed before and entered an unfamiliar room, rather dilapidated and furnished solely with a gigantic chandelier whose crystals inundated the space with a lunar brightness. A downcast man approached me.

"You wouldn't have a match?" he asked me.

I gave him one.

"It could warm the place up a bit, right?" he said to me.

I've just woken up. Much too late, I realize: a first snag, which signals to me that morning has officially started. Turns out I had set the alarm for 3 September . . .

I jump into the furnace without delay. It should be noted that all the power comes from the furnace because the electricity, like the apartment's microclimate or the industrial-scale semaphore—everything here, in fact—runs off central heating. A convenient but costly method: we cycle through furniture several times a month. Once again, I gather up what I come across by chance, several wads of banknotes to ignite the wood, a little acajou bookcase to get the heat going, two doors for the daytime, all while daydreaming about buying a living-room forest, which would simplify everything. I then verify the ignitions and the odometers. I observe with satisfaction that the apartment is maintaining its normal altitude, the light wind from the southwest seems stable, and that though the day's pressure appears rather low, its specific gravity is no cause for concern: the manometer indicates, without possibility of error, that the temperature of my delay is decreasing and that I'm falling one meter every fifteen seconds.

I barely have time to wash the windows, scatter some seeds on the flower carpet in the hallway, and gather up the flying fish that flew in the previous night before grilling up a grasshopper kebab for breakfast.

The warning lights embedded in the walls are already changing from red to green. The express train that connects the kitchen to the Islands has just crossed the hallway in a clamor of wheezing, crushed gravel, and weeping iron. As happens every morning, the vibrations have caused some damage, and a number of broken knickknacks litter the floor. And like every morning, as a measure of caution I check to see that no one has thrown themselves onto the tracks, after which I open the window, then wave the red and gold pennant to signal to the concierge that all is clear. While I'm at it, I shake hands with a fellow tenant passing by the window in a tethered balloon, heading back to the office where he occupies a high-up position.

My wife, meanwhile, calls me back to reality.

"Your head's in the clouds. You forgot to close off the hallway passageway last night."

I tell Mygale that no one goes down that hallway at night and that besides, the last train passes through at ten o'clock. I also let her know that I left the gas valves open and we're none the worse for it. Mygale hears me without comprehending, no opinion ever sways her, she remains trapped within her own logic, that of a simpleton.

As for my son, he emerges from the pipes where he'd spent the night. He brings the haul from his nocturnal fishing into the kitchen. Not much: some corks, a sizeable slug, a metallic rod of little interest, and a scrap of decomposed hemp. Mygale immediately starts marinating it all. Afterward, she'll illuminate the lighthouse she tends to during the day to augment our meager earnings.

My son, our firstborn, leaves after dropping off one of his feet with his mother, who needs to buy him a pair of shoes this morning. Then, equipped with several meters of rope, a supply of oxygen, and a compass, he heads off to school.

"Did you leave me some money?" Mygale asks me.

No, I'd forgotten. I need to use a blowtorch to break open the safe, whose combination I can no longer recall. But I crack it open to no avail: it was in fact the refrigerator, where naturally I find only my suits. The safe itself is impossible to locate. I comb the bathroom wall where we installed it. Finally, Mygale remembers having donated it during the latest collection drive for parents of unemployed orphans. Mygale forgets everything these days. If I wasn't around, we'd really be stuck.

"Careful you don't catch cold down the hall," she tells me by way of avoiding any further discussion.

The fact is that if the kitchen enjoys an almost tropical climate, the hallway is often buffeted by monsoons and snowstorms. Yet, despite its insalubrious climate, it's been a point of convergence for quite a few events in our life. Built forty years before the house, it was part of the work projects undertaken during the dredging of the Suez Canal, which, incidentally, it secretly mirrors. If its significance as a waterway is negligible, its familial importance is considerable. Furthermore, it was in this corridor where my grandfather met his end while fighting tooth and nail to save the apartment from the great tides which carried off the flood barrier, the walls, and a coat rack that year.

Today, however, cold reigns in the hallway, while the living room is experiencing a full thaw, with blocks of ice, and the frozen furniture trapped within, tumbling from the windows. Fortunately, the kitchen was built close to the equator and it's a pleasant environment. I find Mygale there, suntanned, glowing, entirely naked and thrilled to be able to cook an egg in her hand.

Someone rings. As this happens often—doubtless a wrong address—the erupting bell causes the ceiling to collapse.

"Go open it," I tell Mygale, extricating myself from the plaster.

Naturally, there's no one there. It must have been the bald soprano on the fifth floor.

As opening the door proved fruitless, I turn on the radio, which discharges a torrent of warm water over the medium wavelengths. After hastily shaving with my toothbrush, I leave the bathroom, resolved to take on the day with dry efficiency, even though rain was forecast.

All I need to do now is leave the apartment, which automatically folds in on itself and into the closet.

There's quite the commotion in the stairway. On the fourth floor, I can barely skirt by the gawkers watching the changing of the guard. Lower down, I'm caught up in a procession of people stammering inanities as they carry their toys and eunuchs up to the roof to commune more closely with their God. On the second floor, trucks are unloading a shipment of cotton balls into the freight elevator, which is about to haul anchor. The roar of sirens rips through the air. Seagulls frolic in the elevator car, and housewives returning from the market with full mesh bags have to defend themselves from these voracious birds. Occasionally, a dump truck scoops up a tenant and deposits them in the cotton-ball-filled elevator. Customs officers from the river brigade ask people for their papers and search those traveling from the second floor to the lobby. The air is oily, almost opaque. In a corner by the door, a dozen embittered dock workers debate whether to strike. The concierge makes a little pocket money by offering to pilot the elevator, which must shortly traverse the always perilous zone of intermediate floors, where the reefs and wind gusts are particularly treacherous during this season. Certain more enterprising inhabitants have transformed their apartment entryways into storefronts, and merchandise seems to be flying off the shelves. A car labors up the wall of the second floor to unload a swarm of enraptured tourists.

It's a beautiful day, but for those concerned with punctuality, clearing a path through this tumult presents a real challenge. I manage nonetheless and find myself in the lobby. It's snowing there, and the commercial traffic has given way to children playing games. I head toward the commuter elevator that descends to the train from my building.

"Filthy weather, no?" the man punching my ticket says in passing.

It's true. But the concierge is already coming out from his station with a bucket and several towels, determined to polish it.

I step out onto the platform just as a train is pulling in. It's the carriage of the dead, which I take each morning to my job as a sewer employee: my office is right next to the cemetery.

I sit across from the corpse of a young woman, and after several minutes attempt to strike up a conversation. Initially hesitant, she finally accepts a cigarette after asking the other passengers if the smell would bother them. I'm delighted to have come across someone so polite. I ask her how she ended up here, and she tells me. It's a long tale, a whole life story in fact, and not that exciting at the end of the day. But how could I hold that against her? A dead person inspires a certain respect, in spite of everything.

Before heading off, the young woman invites me to visit her one of these days in her vault, which she hasn't yet seen but which is supposed to be charming and excellently situated. I take my leave, kissing my companion's icy hand and wishing her a good night.

I take a steep staircase up to my office. The company where I've been working for several months belongs to the Society of Reunited Sewers, a vast network of official (though underground) offices whose aim is to centralize the frequency patterns and perturbing modulations within every sewer in the city. A task of presumably infinite complexity, as it demands a very large workforce. At any rate, accomplishing it is impossible in practice because there's no electricity, and the regulations prohibit candlelight. This doesn't exempt employees from working the required eight-hour shifts, hours which, incidentally, we have no trouble filling, since we have to factor in the six hours spent fumbling around to locate our assigned desk and the (at minimum) three hours to find the exit in the afternoon.

Today, we are burying the unknown employee who the day before yesterday got stuck in a nook we've always called the storehouse, without realizing that it could in fact permanently store *us* as well. A small diversion in this obscure job that could only appeal to functionaries of moderate ambition. But so it goes—one has to make a living, right?

"ONE HAS TO MAKE A LIVING, right?"

Strange, repeat it often enough and you end up believing it. Make a living—we've beaten the topic to death! Same for a zest for living, a lust for life, and the fear of living. But have we covered the smug tranquility of all those who never thought of living, because no one ever gave them the chance to be born? They've died as well, in fact. And so long ago! You agree with me!

"I do, yes."

"That's what's disturbing. And yet you won't at the very least tell me about your life? Or rather, yes, tell me what you did the day before . . ."

"The day before when?"

"Days don't matter. Where were you the day before? By what right? What lay behind the closed shutters of the first house on the right? And who taught you left from right? Exactly how much did your mother weigh? And the day before, what happened the day before?"

The day before . . . I remember. It was probably 9 October of a year caught between two others, and nothing was going on that day. It wasn't even raining.

But then everything happened all at once, just as the morning paper arrived.

I'm not expecting a letter. I haven't written to myself for a long time, but the concierge comes into my apartment with a mail-bag that she tosses on the floor.

"There's been a mistake," I confidently tell her.

But all these letters bear my name. I pick out several envelopes, the ones with the most unusual headers. Here the Vatican, there the Katanga Mines, the Chemical Union, the SNCF, the Minister of Fine Arts. I clearly remember writing to the Pope ten years ago to wish him a Merry Christmas. But would he reply to me after so long? I open several letters. They are definitely addressed to me. Why? For what reason? No one clues me in. *Dear Monsieur*, say all the letters. *Please accept* ... And I accept, of course, I accept. The editor of a weekly offers me a two million advance for a simple summary of my life. The government asks me to pose for its new bank notes, and the Church wants my silhouette to replace the iconic Christ. Symphonies attempt to tinkle out my name, and presidential advisers offer me the office in exchange for some advice. Couples beg me to officiate their marriage, others want me to perform a baptism, and two ask me to give them extreme unction. Tenants whom I'd never heard of assure me that from now on, they will pay their rent every trimester, and the destitute inform me that they are sending me bread crusts by registered mail, farmers their dairy products, and mothers their baby clothes. Three old women let me know that I am their sole heir and that there's no need to wait for them to die to tap into the fortunes they've cast before me. Six hundred and ten voluntary paratroopers form a death brigade and place themselves under my command.

Who in fact am I? I check my identity card just in case and recognize myself. My photo looks like me. And this card indicates that I am an employee, with no further details. It doesn't really matter anyway. But how to begin sifting through this avalanche of windfalls and propositions? Perhaps with the editor offering me an advance? I go to the address indicated, but I'm told that he has just departed on a cruise and left no message for me. I recall the inheritances from the millionaires but note that they didn't leave me their address. At the bank that offered me an open-ended account with an infinite credit limit, I'm informed that I first have to make an initial deposit of 500,000 francs. The corporate directors eagerly receive me, thanking me for having responded to their offer so quickly and assuring me that I will be hearing from them very shortly. They'll write.

Thankfully, I have just enough money left for a taxi. I arrive at the office. Everything is gray, a gray sunk into the walls and floors. The day alone towers overhead in its full duration, higher than a prison wall.

"You should send us a pneumatic message when you're this late," the department manager tells me.

"The train made a detour."

"Oh? Then deliver this letter to the Minister of Transportation," says the department head to a secretary. "We're going to make an official restitution claim."

I go to the window. I recognize the scene and its bit players. Across from me, a woman sprinkles air over her sixth child in a flowerpot. Next to a porch, a beggar has hung himself to elicit pity. A sewage worker descends into the family vault he has secretly built under the sidewalk and, not far from that, an apathetic street sweeper pushes a river of diamonds into the gutter. On a fifth-floor balcony, two children watch a herd of bison. A concierge is trying to cram a cadaver she's just discovered in the hallway into a trash can when an officer tells her that it's forbidden to put bodies out on the street before nightfall. The same old story. Nothing ever happens outside office windows. Nor inside, for that matter. Maybe something happens within the panes?

The postman enters the mailroom and, along with several letters, removes his large intestine from his bag, which he sets on the large table. The accountants have been counting their fingers for the past month, delighted that they've all arrived at the same result. A secretary has carved her mail into thin slices to make a salad, which she's spiced up with a bit of watercress and is about to dig into with her fork. The young assistant gathers up all the commas littered across the floor with a broom. From a large box of Meccano pieces, a clerk builds a giant inkpot in a decidedly modern style. An editor feeds the hem of her suit into the typewriter. The others entertain themselves the best they can, using whatever means the day has put at their disposal to escape their bleak reality: this one sneezing, that one blowing his nose, another wiping his glasses. Trifling amusements.

It was then that, for no reason at all, I turned on the lights.

One little click and, as if the entire room was connected to a power source, everything changed. The room and facial expressions began to thrum with life; arteries, situations, and seconds swelled with various fluids. The calendar lost fifteen grams in one minute; the central heating let out strident whines from all its pipes, the ceiling dissolved into a single mass of foam from which exploding light bulbs rained down. Assaulted by ten million electrodes, boredom let fly an ecstatic cry, a burst of laughter whose force blew apart the entire accounting department and half of shipping. The fan started tearing apart the air so violently that it was shredded into long strips, blood trailing in its wake. Tables sunk into the floor, dragging down the crying wretches who, having been attached to the company for too long, couldn't manage to free themselves. The greater part of the company's files had, after some final crinkling, been reduced to a churning foam in which two particularly zealous assistant managers drowned trying to ascertain how the company could profit from this froth.

A department head entered the room and noticed the light.

"Who turned it on?" he asked.

I stepped forward.

"Do you want to end up on the scaffold?"

He asked me to follow him, leading me into another room.

An enormous grindstone made of wood, steel, and rock was slowly turning around a rough axis. Two shirtless men were bound to this grindstone. They were walking, limp wrecks covered in sweat, backs lined with lash marks, clothes in tatters.

"I'm sorry," said the department head to me, "but I've got to put my foot down."

He tied me to a beam after having secured my wrists and ankles to a heavy chain. He proceeded to remove my coat, my tie, and then my shirt.

"Turn," screamed a man whose whip came down between my shoulders.

I started to walk. The stone began to creak, grinding out sawdust. I had noticed a small plate full of shavings in the corner of the hall off the lobby and always wondered about it. Now I knew.

The days pass. The grindstone perpetually turns. We follow it. Or we push it. We no longer know. We turn. We try to catch up. We grind the darkness, time, and sawdust. When we ask for water, the man with the whip spits in our faces. When we ask to eat, he thrusts our heads into a bowl of sawdust. When we ask for fresh air, he walks behind us with a fan.

Fortunately, the petite secretary who types up the correspondence works next to the grindstone. She has a nice tan from the sunlight of resignation. She is hot and hard, soft and silky, and every three minutes the strong scent of her body wafts over us. At a certain point in the circle we trace, I can see her legs, her thighs, and even her bare stomach when the weather is clear. She is blonde and brunette, somber and blissful. Sometimes I reach out my hand and take one of her letters as I pass. I read it; it distracts me. On my rounds, the young girl occasionally leans toward me, and I caress her breasts. I distract her; this consoles me. With every turn of the wheel, every three minutes, we exchange words. I turn so that I can talk to her. I keep on turning only for that.

"You are vertigo. My head spins from seeing you spinning like that through my life."

"You are commerce. I like the way your stomach creases when you strike a vowel."

"You have beautiful feet. I could stay here for hours watching the tendons go taut when you put one foot in front of the other."

"You are as beautiful as a typewriter. So shapely and smooth. You are the flesh of metal, the softness of steel chrome, the finish on a piece of machinery."

"You are beautiful, like the sawdust you grind. You are my sandy beach on the shore of despair, the movement of the waves, the color of my soul's waves."

"I love you as I hate the fatigue that breaks my back."

"I love you as I hate the 'warm regards' that flow from my fingers."

"I want to hear you cry in me the way this grindstone does."

"I want to feel you striking me the way your fingers strike the typewriter keys."

"The steel arm I push is the ghastly analogue of your body I ravage in slow motion."

"The white page on which I scribble words is your body's mirage in which I drown."

"You are my impossible within reach."

"You are my possible just beyond my grasp."

"Our three minutes of separation seem like hours, years."

"I forget you and then rediscover you as if you had never existed."

"Hello, my third minute."

"Good night, my cooling fan."

"I love you, my intermittent mirage."

"I long for you, my eternal curve."

"Enough talking."

"Speak to me."

"Tap away."

"Turn."

"I turn you."

"I tap you."

"I adorn you."

"I trap you."

"I return you."

"I retrap you."

"I turn you away."

"I am you."

"I am me."

"I am us."

"We are, thus we turn."

And then, despite these sentiments, the inevitable occurred: I ended up inventing the principle of the rolling circle, the cogwheel, gears, steam, mechanical power. I alert management. They congratulate me, granting me a certificate and a position as a correspondence writer.

I returned to the office one fine spring morning. It was a nice, dry day, the lilacs were singing in the invoices, the squirrels emerged from their drawers, and the half-naked employees sang as they gathered the fruits of their winter labor, which the department heads piled into summer baskets that their assistants carried off to the autumn presses.

I was back at it. Nothing can definitively happen to you once you've joined an office staff.

The tattered liabilities are crawling across a chart of the company's financial earnings, which had shot out of the frame, quick as lightning, to impale a communications supervisor. Two firefighters have just come to the window to extinguish a lit cigarette in the ashtray. The telephone occasionally picks itself up and wanders around. An accountant examines the imponderables of the catalog sales figures under a microscope, and managers open all the drawers to free young women who emerge unfazed, adjusting their stockings. Having transformed into a mare, a secretary, drunkenly ecstatic from being whipped and ridden, hitches herself to a large oak desk, which she pulls toward the exit, arching her haunches, foaming at the mouth, on all fours, breasts taut, mane unfurled. Another, having rediscovered her lost faith, has nailed herself to a cross, and ten employees try in vain to stack themselves as high as this living statue contorted in a posture brimming with mysticism and obscenity.

The director finally arrives. Dressed in a first communion blue, he starts off by crying because someone broke the wheel of his mechanical rabbit. We console him by sending a clerk to find him a police uniform. He then pulls himself together, slaps an employee who raised his head without so much as asking permission, telephones the station to denounce another worker who had stained his fingers filling an inkpot, then heads to my desk and snatches up two letters lying on it.

"Two letters in one month," he says to me. "Your production is hardly satisfactory. I'm wondering if I should . . ."

In a flash, I find myself in another room, much darker and sparer. A large table is in the center, cleared as if awaiting a cadaver to be dissected. The light falls on this surface alone, no reflections elsewhere. At the four corners of the table, which seems to be suspended over a large hole, are wristless hands, immobile in their wait for prey.

All of a sudden, a clerk distributes a batch of fliers to the hands, simultaneously inciting hunger and anger. Like the other hands, mine break into an epileptic fit and fall upon the fliers, which we must fold in quarters. Nothing exists other than this imperative. We can't help ourselves. We are nothing but severed hands, which another employee will surely return to a closet after work. We are reduced to lowly little mollusks capable only of crablike scuttling and blotting, embossing, cutting paper, knitting and sweeping, wholly independent, roaming larva making their own way in the world.

Hours pass by, or perhaps minutes.

Something abruptly shifts and stirs within me. I'm flooded with charges of insight and genius, exploding like grenades. I must, I want to, I will create something. I get up, ask my department head for permission to step out for a bit.

I leave. It's my lucky day. I learn from the newspapers that I have just received the Nobel Prize for folding fliers. I treat myself to a cigarette and instantly conjure one that lights without producing any smoke. My next breakthrough is stralte, the veritable fifth element that is impossible to describe in words. The creative instinct swells my veins, fortune shines upon me once more, and I receive the Prix Renaudot, as well as the Goncourt, without ever having written anything. I seize the moment by developing a tactile screen exclusively for blind people, and then inventing a radiator that plays church music and whose mystic intensity varies according to the heat of the sacred fire. After swimming underwater across the Manche, all while memorizing the phone directory of the chronically unreachable, I take a couple hours to compose a history of the twenty-first century, describing with sadistic relish the two future wars which humankind will vainly try to avoid. I drop by the planet Kaos for a coffee crème and, with several pencil strokes, sketch out an astral paltralogic based on the Aldephore principle. For the second time that morning, I receive the Nobel Prize, and an Oscar as well. I send my double as a proxy to Sweden and my reflection to the United States, while, with the help of some tokens I found in an old game box, I fabricate a businessman's brain that one can disassemble after the workday in a few seconds. I escape to a deserted island to relax, but my luck has preceded me there: she welcomes me with open arms and wraps them around me.

Wishing to escape, I jump into a bottomless canoe and attempt to cross the Atlantic without a paddle, without a compass, without a tiller; a mysterious current sweeps me up and, with the speed of a cruise ship sailing on calm, flat seas, deposits me on an enchanted beach in Florida, where I am kept, under armed guard, at a palace at the State's expense, showered with women, fruit, and flowers. I plunge into the poisonous swamps of the Amazonian jungle, resolved to lose my way, but I make it back from this death-defying jaunt via a picturesque little path that shields me from the jungle's dangers as if I were in a garden, no need even to duck a hanging branch. I bring back a dozen butterflies and a herbarium.

It occurs to me that I'm going to call attention to myself, and that this is going to cost me my job. It's time to return to the office, where my absence must have been noticed. Without further delay, I'm back at my worktable. There are still fliers to fold.

"They tell me you're a fast, solid worker," the director says to me after embracing me and handing me various awards. "I've decided to entrust you with a more important job."

And indeed, three employees are looking at me. They seem to be awaiting my orders.

I direct one of them to write up a list of three thousand imaginary addresses for the following morning, threatening immediate dismissal if even one address actually exists. I ask another to slip ten thousand identical fliers into ten thousand envelopes addressed to the firm's director, all to be delivered by the same messenger. I'm about to ask the third to count the commas in the morning mail when I notice the director's face beneath his disguise as a humble employee. He informs me that he has indeed received the ten thousand fliers that same morning and apologizes for not yet having had the time to read them.

I cut him short, telling him that his excuses are wasting my time. He then checks his watch, and, in compensation for these lost minutes, writes me a check for 300,000 francs. I tell him that he has always been stingy and will never change; he attempts a smile, fails, brings out a grinning mask from his pocket, dons it, and leaves the room in silence, taking with him the partitions, the ceiling, and the floor.

Only one parquet square remains, along with some familiar furniture arranged on this last patch. They are in fact from my apartment. Do I therefore live here? In the open air? But it's undeniable: I live in a furnished square. And a spacious one to boot.

Someone rings at the square's large gate. I go to open it. I recognize this woman. I wasn't expecting her tonight, but I've actually been living with Mygale for several years and, if my memory serves, we have a child. He's also there. I'm delighted: I thought I forgot him on a train platform last year.

"Have you eaten?" asks Mygale.

I tell her no.

"How do you take your water?" she asks. "With water or oil?"

"With water," I reply to facilitate matters. Half-heartedly, as I don't share Mygale's taste for simple dishes. But how could I reproach her? For me, trapped in a world teeming with madmen, Mygale represents fixity, refusal, waiting, truth. She takes off her outer face and the other appears, the one I prefer, features hardened, almost frozen but also nervy, her eyes deep-set within her sockets but wide open, her pupils melting within an imageless dream.

"I did three minutes of housework this morning," she tells me.

I congratulate her: the four sides of the alley have been dusted and the gravel raked with care. No pieces of wood or greasy papers are lying around. The clothes are all hanging on trees. The grass on the carpet appears freshly repainted. And the tree leaves, if not all ironed to perfection, are nevertheless very neat.

"We'll have to remember to buy naphthalene," says Mygale. "I found another bat in my furs."

"You'll have to remember," I tell her.

"Yes, remind me. I'll handle it."

Around ten o'clock, there's another ring at the gate. It's the mailman delivering a pneumatic letter. The people at the bank are very surprised about my prolonged absence. I'm surprised as well, for I didn't know I was employed in a bank. I look over my planner. Nothing scheduled for today. Tomorrow doesn't appear in the book. Moving on to Wednesday, then. I see that it's a holiday. A lucky break. That takes us to Sunday, which, for reasons unknown to me, has been moved forward this week. And no notes anywhere else. Not that I ever write anything in my planners. I even end up wondering whether I really have a planner. I flip through it once more. Could this actually be a pencil I have in my hands? But can one flip through a pencil?

"Are you employed at the moment?" Mygale asks.

"Of course. What do you think we're living on?"

"I don't know. I thought you've been out of work for four years."

I'm not surprised by her reply. Mygale is never surprised either. Nothing surprises us. At any rate, it's quite rare for Mygale to ask me a question. By now she is completely devoid of any curiosity, to such an extent that she has no idea how old I am or who I am. I'm not sure she's looked at me yet. Just like the cats, Mygale is curled up in her favorite corner, always the same. I've never seen her otherwise. Her greatest pleasure is to roll up into a ball, curled up with her gaze directed inward, huddled around her inertial force. Tonight, though, she is exceptionally talkative—that's the third question she's asked. Two hours later, she asks me again what I'm working on at the moment.

"The same old stuff," I tell her, "under different names."

It was only much later that she asked me if I liked my work. In the meantime, I'd already changed jobs thirty-two times. But my answer hadn't changed.

Therefore, to avoid answering again, I go to check that the gate is firmly shut. I turn off the gas lights and the big central streetlamp.

"The cleaning lady is coming tomorrow," Mygale says. "She's going to burn all the dead leaves and give everything a thorough raking."

"It's cold," I note.

"Maybe you didn't shut the gate all the way?"

It's possible, yes.

Before putting it back in my pocket, I discreetly check my calendar. It's far from reassuring: a bad year. Best to outrun it.

That's what I decide to do.

IT'S OFTEN SAID that no one can escape their fate. I was indeed soon caught, and the attempt cost me two years in the penal colony. Because of my marital status, I was assigned to an embroidery hard labor camp. The prisoners had it relatively easy there, some spinning wool, others designing tapestries they would sell to the neighboring convent, which was secretly connected to the penitentiary via a cellar that became a pleasure den for the convicts.

By the time I got out, I was exhausted from the nuns' insatiable desire for debauchery, a few pounds heavier but holding a patent for an embroidery machine, which proved quite useful down the line.

"Where have you been all this time?" Mygale asks me. "Dinner's been waiting."

I notice that the apartment is in a sorry state. The hallway has collapsed, and we now have a permanent window into the lives of the fourth-floor residents.

"This hole is dangerous," I say.

"Yeah, the kid falls in sometime," Mygale tells me.

In the kitchen, a mass of rust, congealed fat, and broken porcelain sits atop a graveyard of greasy papers. It's nothing more than a wasteland where the tenants have gotten into the habit of tossing their trash. The bedroom is even more dreadful: it now has only two dimensions. Mygale explains that she had to economize during my absence and had no choice but to sacrifice the third. The bed rests on a little island of floorboards threatening to collapse at any moment.

"It looks like it's held together by magic."

"It's holding," says Mygale. "I put a little glue on one side of the bed. I'm going to take a bath," she adds.

When she reemerged, she was ten years younger and thus didn't recognize me: after all, we'd only been married for eighteen months.

"What are you doing here?" she asked.

"My apologies," I replied, flustered.

Grabbing a suitcase lying around, I opened the door and entered another hallway, a much longer one. An emergency passage, surely, or simply an extension. And with such low ceilings, and so dark. Making my way through was quite an ordeal . . . In certain spots, the floor almost touched the ceiling, and you had to crawl, always looking out for gaping holes in the floor. From time to time, something would brush over my legs, subterranean larvae perhaps, or mammalian spiders crawling from one wall to the other. It often rained; an apartment storm also broke out, but it was minor. A tempest of dead leaves followed in its wake. Not to mention the minor nuisances, like the concierge who followed me for seven kilometers to tell me that I could have at least wiped my feet before entering.

And then there was that suitcase, which grew heavier and heavier though it had been empty when I left the apartment. I opened it under the glow of an indoor streetlamp: it was filled with water. The humidity, no doubt. I emptied it, but it gradually refilled as soon as I set off again.

When I heard that loud din, I thought I'd finally made it through. It was only a subway tunnel intersecting the hallway, with no signage in sight. I narrowly escaped death.

I was growing increasingly discouraged when I spotted a glimmer of light. After almost taking a wrong turn into the gas pipes, the beam from a flashlight landed squarely on my face. I emerged into the gaudily opulent ballroom of a grand hotel.

"Goodbye, sir. We look forward to seeing you soon," the porter said.

He opened the door for me and indicated the pallid sidewalk along a main drag.

I recognized this city. I especially remembered the nights I had spent in my apartment there after my shifts at the PTT:[2] that year, I had gotten into the habit of stealing several dozen letters from the office each night to bring home and personally answer, overwhelmed by a job that demanded my full attention. The episode ended badly, but I enjoyed the city itself quite a bit. It really had everything one could want: a well-tended sky, central heating all summer long, a children's slaughterhouse, and thirty-eight movie houses where each night several beasts were thrown to the Christians.

Nothing had changed. Some streets had slightly shifted toward the city center after the storms of 27. And the day is in full swing. Antitubercular stamps are flying off the shelves at charity sales, while tuberculosis, charitable in its own right, is already turning the flesh of those buying them gangrenous. The big funeral companies pay bums to publicly perform death throes as part of an advertising campaign. Processions crowd the sidewalk amid the luxuriant aroma of incense, while forlorn prostitutes dressed in black panhandle to support disinherited grandfathers. Near the train station, a contingent of paralyzed priests returns from a pilgrimage to Lourdes, from which they had set out in excellent health. Thousands of crocheted doors snare millions of passersby, and sorters separate the buyers from the browsers, whom machines hasten to cut up into retail objects: gloved hands, hats (with heads available on a trial basis), shirts with torsos, tendons and ties, fabrics and flesh, pieces hurriedly offered up to hordes of fashion lovers seeking a makeover or to round out their personality.

A city, in sum, like any other. What else to do here but sell in order to buy, resell, and rebuy? What should I become? A sales rep, seeing as I had a suitcase. It's pointless to bring along samples as I'm not representing any company. I've made my decision, even though I know that the sales rep business doesn't suit me. My powers of persuasion are nil. Usually, I buy the very goods I'm hawking. Even if I ultimately snatch them up at a discounted price at the end of the day, that's a lot of hassle for no gain.

My first bit of bad luck arrives right off the bat at 9am. A cop stops me.

"No selling allowed on this street," he tells me. "Even days only."

I move to another street. At 9:15, my suitcase bumps into the freshly painted fender of a car parked too close to the curb. I have to step in to pry them apart. Then, I lose a glove and realize I left one of my fingers in it. The day's not looking good at all.

And supposing I got to work? Where to start? A butcher shop? Why not? A calf head in a window, a lemon between its teeth, seems to be soliciting me. I enter the store and offer ball bearings at a price that no competitor could match. I'm turned down. Next, I go into a haberdashery, where I present fitted parts for radiators, then a bookstore where I claim to represent a large manufacturer of braided shoelaces. They send me packing again.

Business isn't booming over here. I cross the street and walk into a repair shop, where demand is just as low: things are no better on this side. It's clear I should try another neighborhood. As there's no recapturing lost time, I try to sell railing supports to a police officer and aeronautic materials to a prostitute on the walk over. All for naught. Either I'm doing something wrong, or my merchandise is worthless.

Is it a bad seller's market? Perhaps. But what about the buy side? To find out, I go into several stores and acquire, successively and without difficulty, a pack of cigarettes, a slice of ham, and 100 grams of nails. I'm warmly received everywhere. There's no problem with purchasing things, which means selling must be possible. Energized, I give it another go. I try to offload one standard-measure meter, a cube of fresh air, a tube of want-some-of-this, and a slice of easy-to-cut. All to no avail, despite my pitches. I come to the conclusion that there's a glaring discrepancy between the seller's and buyer's markets.

If I want to keep on being a sales rep, best to change eras. I make inquiries at the Tourism Office, where I'm informed that in 37, not very far from here, there's an inverse financial crisis. That's what I need. I just have to take the bus to the outskirts and get off at the first stop after the terminus. I'm there in twenty minutes.

The crisis is raging, the franc has risen considerably, and life there is but a permanent resplendence shimmering with billions of gold and platinum flecks.

I check the time. Ten o'clock. I plan on staying one hour and taking the 10:55 back to 26.

One hour should suffice, I imagine. But what should I do? Roam the streets gathering money? That would be exploiting the situation. Surely it's time to prove that I'm just as capable of making a future for myself in 37 as I was in 26. I head into a commercial building and push open the first door I see. The latch comes off in my hand: it's made of gold, a bonus offered to every visitor. I'm ushered in with the utmost haste, presented with an honorary check to thank me for having solicited on their premises, and promised an official ceremony that very night. The director saw fit to receive me in formal attire. It must have been years since he'd laid eyes on a salesman. I inform him that I'm the representative for an important agricultural machinery manufacturer, and he assures me he's supremely interested in this sector, along with everything related to human culture.

"I'm required to sell them in batches of 5,000," I tell him, "on top of an equivalent number of repair units in case of mechanical failures. Which, frankly, happen often."

"Perfect, perfect," the director replies. "I believe in unreliable equipment."

"I should also let you know that I can't promise a delivery date earlier than ten years from now."

"No matter. Time works *for* us. Each minute lost entails seconds, which yield heaps of millions. One can only imagine how much we'd make if we stalled for time. The longer your delays, the better it suits me. Oh, and these machines, I'd appreciate it if you delivered them in pieces if possible. That would allow us to incur additional fees to assemble them."

"Understood. Can you write me a check?"

"Imagine that! I'll pay you in cash right away. Please tell me this machinery of yours is expensive, at least? Our prices will be different, at any rate. I can only pay you by the kilo."

I show him my suitcase. The director appears skeptical.

"Not a lot will fit in there," he tells me. "Well, we'll find a way to stuff it all in. You don't sell floodlights by chance? I've been looking for a way to illuminate the public for years."

I reply that I'm sorry, but that I really don't . . .

"No matter. I'll order 1,200. You'll deliver them fictitiously, at the same time as the tractors."

That's how I made my first several million. A fortune that, it should be noted, didn't last long. Several minutes later, I made the mistake of buying a stamp that cost me 340 million: postage rates had risen that morning. Then I drank a coffee that was even more expensive, sugar having become a rare commodity since the previous day. Soon I only had enough left to get back on my feet. Which was easy.

I went into a butcher's shop, where I declared to the owner that I had opened a charitable fund for talentless writers and that I was soliciting every human being for help. He not only found the plan excellent but ushered me into the salon without making me wait in the shop among its golden calves and the smoked wads of cash that hung from the ceiling.

"I myself had writerly ambitions," the butcher confessed. "Even my wife had proclivities. But what's there to say? Not enough time. Ultimately, we content ourselves with buying books."

And indeed, behind several dancers and a bronze archer, three ornamental shells, an ashtray embossed with a licentious inscription, and a Directoire-style turntable stretched a magnificent glass-front bookcase of Polynesian wood crammed with at least three thousand volumes bound in Moroccan leather, composing a tableau of undeniable austerity.

"You see . . . they're all there," this bibliophile told me: "the authors I love and reread constantly—Kafka, Cioran, Ionesco, Melville, Dostoyevsky, Sternberg, Lautréamont, Beckett, Joyce, Lovecraft, Céline, and the rest. All original editions. I like beautiful writing, but I appreciate beautiful bindings just as much. It's the same with nice cuts of meat: I easily devour two and half books a day, three if they're avant-garde. I have a passion for the fiery ones, the tormented souls . . . This is for the writers with no talent, you were saying? Are there really any? Anyway, we'll sort that out."

I left with my suitcase full of 100,000-franc bills. Moreover, the butcher's wife insisted on giving me a calf's foot. It was ten to eleven. Time to catch the bus back.

Upon arriving at the 26 station, I noticed that I'd forgotten my suitcase in 37. In return, the Suitcase Compensation Office granted me the sum of 450 francs. That wasn't enough to get me past tomorrow. My only remaining hope was to secure an inheritance. I had rubbed out a whole branch of my family with this in mind, but to no avail: the money always went to someone else, never me. I did still have one centenarian grandmother in the area who had a considerable fortune, but she was growing younger by the day. Everything led me to believe that our trajectories would intersect at around forty years of age, and that she'd end up becoming my inheritor.

I could see no other choice but to drop the plan. I found Mygale in a small furnished flat next to the dried-out canal.

"You didn't get my letter at the office?" she asks.

"What office?"

"Oh well, the letter will come back."

"You put the return address on?"

"They know me in the neighborhood. Look, I bought myself a Bible. You should read the Old Testament. It's very interesting. Especially in Hebrew. And then, you know, it reads backwards, which is much more fun . . ."

What a revelation! I'm seeing a way out of this impasse.

Straight away, I test out my theory. Heading out the door, I come across a funeral procession returning from the cemetery to retrace the deceased's path back through his death throes, illness, negligence. It's 6:10 according to a sliding clock. It's still too late to find work, the offices have already closed; but soon, around 5:30, it'll be easy to land a job. Unfortunately, I can't understand a word of what people are saying around me. It must be because of the inverted syllables. However, I easily grasp the jokes of three Hungarian tourists I meet in front of a hotel.

A four in the afternoon, I set to work straight away but find myself in a company that has yet to be created. Truly discouraging. Might as well go back home. My days are worthless, no matter which end I start from.

APART FROM THE DAYS, there are the nights, especially the nights of full daylight, all the more lugubrious because their atmosphere is nothing but a blanket of chloroform, a gigantic sugary quilt. There are also nights in which it is impossible to distinguish between the Earth and the void, the past and the future, those nights one seeks to escape while puzzling over which secret portal led there. And then there are those nights seeming to bridge familiar landscapes and ones that are anonymous, featureless, glacial.

I find myself in precisely such surroundings. But where exactly am I? Everywhere, it seems. What time is it? And why this feeling that I'll be forever outside of time? My first order of business is to escape, for I am alive. I'm sure of it. If I were dead, I'd know it. I move through a heap of confused scenery, a series of tableaus, fragmented though not in tatters, the whole tied together by blurred backdrops or separated by dark hollows that are doubtless gaps in my memory.

I've already run into Mygale several times. She's busy reading and doesn't acknowledge my presence, as if she had sunk into the profound depths of a massive red armchair. I also recognize a business selling air-conditioned rooms where I used to be a bookkeeper. And sections of the road flowing into an apartment I'd moved out of ten years ago. A small public square I have no memory of sprouts up in the middle of a newsroom in which I had pulled quite a few all-nighters. I occasionally meet familiar characters, but I can't understand anything they say to me.

I run into Mygale once again. She is living in all the apartments we had vacated, and at the same time living in our current one. I stop in front of her chair. Behind me, a young woman is typing. To my left, I recognize a rural landscape whose dense fog evokes a memory of dreary, sunless vacations.

"Mygale," I say, to no effect. One of us is dead to the other, and yet we're both alive. But where? Which of us is a reflection, a shadow? I turn back and see that the secretary who had been typing has been replaced by a myopic editor. The years are passing quickly today. I pick up an inkpot, I see it, I feel it in my hand, but I also see it on the table, as if I hadn't grabbed it. This inkpot exists in two worlds, the one I inhabit and another. How do I know which is real? As usual, I throw up my hands. I'm about to step into the street on my right when I bump into an enormous table set with one lone plate, which holds a fruit compote that smells to me like tripe.

"Eat," my father tells me.

The compote looks like a gluey planet, just a shallow mud puddle. It's riddled with minuscule erupting volcanoes. It's smoking, bubbling, coated with boiling lava. You'd swear it contained a bunch of larvae belching out bubbles of the drowned.

"Eat," repeats my father.

The spoon I've just grabbed falls from my hand, hits the floor. From the ringing, it sounds as if the spoon had tumbled into an abyss and shattered an entire city of crystal to bits. From this impact, thousands of new bacteria materialize in the plate of compote. The serving has doubled in size. It's a compote governed by the laws of acoustics, a compote of the most dangerous kind.

"You're eating, right?" my father continues.

There must be some mix-up. I've slipped back into the past, yes, but I'm too old now to relive that period. I'm no longer eleven, and I could crush my father with my bare hands.

"Eat," says a voice.

It's no longer the voice of my father, but an anonymous voice, indifferent, the voice of all the invisible faces that tirelessly work the streets of life barking out commands.

"Eat," it says. "Stop eating. Have a sip. Get up. Go to bed. Work. Stand up straight. Take me. Get out of here. Come here. Stay with me tonight. Bury your head in your arms. Close your legs. Work. Eat. Look me in the eye. Push it in. Again. Faster. Finish the page. Lift your head. Forward march. Let's go now. Eat. Drop it. Sit up straight. Put down your book. Take off. Talk to me."

These commands—precise, geometric, hardened by time, scorched by the light years and yet human despite it all—have crossed millions of barriers, oceans, and galaxies to descend upon me. Why choose me, me alone, as a point of convergence? If only I could take this eloquence and wring its neck, but how? By screaming, perhaps. Yelling, yes, I'm about to yell louder than an alarm sounding for a world on the brink of collapse, when I observe that someone is finally approaching me. A passerby. He's dressed entirely in black, a mourning tie against a black shirt, with black gloves. His face, though, is pale.

"Can you believe this weather?" he asks me. "You'd best flee," he adds.

He's probably right. One should always flee. This is a trap, a false night in which I mistakenly fell asleep, and which has ensnared me in a web of pursuit without visible pursuers. I am clearly being pursued, but by what? I run and find myself once more in front of the fruit compote, this time on the other side of the table. Have

I therefore reached the reverse side of matter? I must say it looks exactly like the other side. This time, however, I take the plate and hurl it against the wall with all my strength. The compote drips down, reaches the floor, and starts to bubble once more; it swells in size and then gradually slackens like a slime-filled slug. It moves forward and crawls over to the table legs, which it sucks on, slowly. The ingested wood causes it to grow, and it turns to me, fixing me in all its mute mass.

"Eat," yells my father, this time addressing the compote.

I run away. Guards, moving on the double, approach me. They all look alike.

"Where is he?" one of them asks me.

"Over there," I say, and they hurry off down an empty hallway.

Farther on, I come across a group of children, also moving on the double.

"We'll get you," screams one of the children as he runs by.

Luckily, a worker arrives and, in a matter of seconds, installs a door in the air and opens it.

"Quick, through there," he tells me.

I enter a high-ceilinged room filled with people. Everyone is talking, but in hushed tones. A well-dressed man takes me by the arm and leads me to a corner.

"Your case is going poorly," he confides. "But you mustn't give up hope. I'm going to get you out of hard labor. We'll get you capital punishment, I promise. Trust me."

After advising me to maintain the utmost discretion, he walks away.

"I'll furnish you with definitive proof that my client is guilty," he suddenly screams.

But no one pays attention.

"A glass of champagne?" asks a valet holding out a tray.

I was looking for the exit when a doctor approached me to ask if I wasn't in too much pain. I told him no.

"This'll make you feel even better," he told me as he handcuffed me to a radiator.

"And take a pill if the pain ever returns," he added.

Moved to pity, a little girl offered me an orange. I thanked her and offered it to her little sister. The orange exploded and claimed twelve victims. No material damage though, thankfully.

Just then, one of my bosses to whom I had submitted my resignation ten or so years earlier came over to tell me that he was expecting my memo by end of day.

"You can see very well that I'm not available," I told him.

"Always an excuse," he responded. "I won't pay them any mind, I'm warning you."

A little later, a plumber came to take out the radiator, which had grown blazing hot, and replace it with a cool mirrored wardrobe, which forced them to unchain me from the pipes. I took this opportunity to seek out the information I needed from a young lady sitting behind a small counter.

"I'm sorry to bother you, mademoiselle, but is this day officially recorded on the calendar?"

She consulted her records.

"Yes, sir. It's even numbered. And with a print run of 365, according to what I see here."

"So, like last year then?"

"Precisely. But this year, we can guarantee you a seaquake, which the agency will provide in September."

“And I imagine it’s possible to secure a visa to change the year?”

“You’d have to make a request. Please fill out this form. Can I see your papers?”

I passed her my identity card, brushing her hand in doing so. The hand felt quite rough to me. In fact, the young woman had transformed into an individual whose appearance struck me as far from unthreatening. He was fixing me with an unforgiving stare.

“Your name,” he said to me, “doesn’t resemble your photo.”

“They weren’t taken the same day.”

“Yes, the name is much less distinct. It could be quite ambiguous, I reckon.”

“I’m very sorry.”

“So am I. For you. These things can take you far.”

He showed me through a wooden gate and into a room where an inspector pointed me to a chair.

“No, not that one, that one. That one’s a fake chair. Everything’s fake here. Whatever it takes . . . or fakes!” he concluded, laughing. But his grave expression soon returned.

“Do you recognize this ticket?” he asked me, holding up a metro pass.

I replied that it was a metro ticket.

“No, it’s *your* metro ticket. And I can prove it: this ticket is punched on the wrong side. Why? Because it was held out the right side up to the agent who, fatally, flipped it over to be punched. Now, you took this extremely personally.”

“You think so?”

“I’m sure of it. Even your name is suspicious. Everyone knows there are two ls in the plural. Now, the victim no longer had a name when she was killed. Based on this, and knowing that the killer took the service stairs, it’s easy to deduce that the killer’s name could be none other than yours. Understand?”

He got up, walked around the room, picked up a ruler and violently threw it at the window, then turned to me.

"So, do you confess?" he said, giving me a slap.

I confessed to the metro incident.

"Perfect," continued the inspector, offering me his hand. "This admission works in your favor. It will be taken into account later, during the trial."

When he asked me if I had anything else to tell him, I replied that if my life interested him, I could recount it to the last detail.

"Excellent. If you would, write it all down and send it to me in the mail as soon as possible. Even lightly fictionalized, if you prefer. We're swamped at the moment, but I'll read your manuscript myself with the utmost pleasure."

I thanked him, he burst into tears, and I consoled him. He expressed his gratitude and offered me a cup of tea; I thanked him again, and he almost started sobbing once more; exasperated, I treated him like the little worm he was. After that, he returned to his suspicious inspector persona, but, when he saw that the broken window had been replaced, he mistook me for the glassworker and proceeded to hand me a 1,000-franc note.

"Nice work," he told me. "You're a skilled craftsman."

He finally sent me off after handing me his card.

I found myself in a room identical to the one I had just left, and the inspector who received me resembled the other one in every respect. A twin brother in a twin room: just my luck.

"So, you're confessing?" he asked me.

Seeing no clear way out of this, I said nothing. He picked up a little bell and gave it a quick shake. A priest in full mass garb entered the office.

"You've got the wrong door, Father," the inspector told him.

"All doors lead to God," replied the priest.

We had to pummel him to get rid of him.

"So," the inspector resumed, ". . . the corpse? What did you do with it?"

The corpse?

"Which corpse?"

"So there were several?" marveled the inspector. "That changes everything. But to simplify things, let's say there were four. I'll knock off one because that's your family allowance by law. I'll eliminate a second by giving you the benefit of the doubt. And the third retroactively via said benefit. But the fourth? What did you do with it?"

Indeed, what could I have done with that corpse I left one day in the hotel room bed? I had returned the following day: that I remembered. I had taken a cab and we, the corpse and I, had gone to the movies. Then we'd spent several hours in a nightclub. At dawn, we had even visited the cemetery to settle on a headstone style. After that, it's all a blank. I must have lost it in the metro.

"You've forgotten the whole thing, haven't you?" suggested the inspector. "It's so much easier that way."

I had to admit this was the case.

"I'm going to refresh your memory," the inspector continued. "One morning, you wake up with a start and realize that your alarm clock hasn't gone off. It's already 9:30, and you're in danger of losing your job. You leave your room without eating breakfast and, before getting on the bus, notice that your shoelaces are untied. What do you do?"

"I stop to tie them."

"Exactly. And it's upon seeing those laces that you think to strangle her."

"Who?"

"Come now, it doesn't matter. The victim is of little consequence in this case. What concerns us here is your mental process. Anyone will do, since murder is now your idée fixe. That's when you see her, the woman who will become your victim."

It was true. I didn't hesitate for one instant. Seeing her walk by, I told myself that death would suit her very well. She had large, glassy eyes, like two swampy puddles. Moreover, she was always smiling. But how could they have found her corpse when I had sewed it up entirely into another body?

"You're wondering how we managed to find the body, right?" the inspector said. "As it happens, we haven't found it. That's precisely what points to you. Let's consider it logically: if you hadn't killed her, you'd have had no reason to hide the body, and we would have found it. Therefore, since we did not find it, you must have killed her. Crystal clear, no?"

"No body, no proof."

"You're wasting your time. Confess, it'll be easier that way."

He signaled to the court clerk, who prepared to take notes. The inspector then asked me a first question, which I answered without hesitation. He asked a second question, to which I replied just as quickly. At that moment, the bailiff intervened and asked a question himself. I responded without thinking twice. The clerk, who grew pensive at my answer, stopped taking notes. The inspector took the blotter and set about transcribing my statement. The clerk asked another question that left me puzzled. But the inspector, keen to make himself useful, soon answered it himself. Deeming his reply ambiguous, the clerk slapped him a couple times. An amateur of judo, the inspector responded by storming the Bastille, clarifying his answer as he did so.

I left them to their interrogation and headed back out to the street.

"Choose a career," read an enormous poster in which a male torso shielded a woman, three children, and a bathroom with its muscles. Choose a career? It was actually time to get on it.

Feeling good, I decided to tackle this whole job thing and pursue a career in management. I thus showed up at a firm, where a supervisor adopted a solemn air when, by way of background, I declared that I'd just gotten out of prison.

"State prison?" he asked, visibly impressed.

"State, yes."

"Perfect, perfect. We also work with the state. You were a common law prisoner?"

"No, civil law."

"Fine, fine. You finished college, I take it?"

"I'm finished with everything."

"Certificates?"

"A blackmailing diploma from the Conservatory and a deserter citation from the infantry."

"You are quite articulate as well. Is your handwriting also up to par?"

"I was a calligrapher assigned to the account of an intergalactic navigation company."

"Any knowledge of accounting?"

"A bit, yes. But only up to seven."

"Can you type?"

"Certainly. I can operate a washing machine as well, and also have some knowledge of surreptitious tretanetics."

"That'll prove very useful here. You must think me quite nosy, but the work that you'll be doing requires a solid foundation. I believe, incidentally, that your salary will be, let's say 750,000 francs a month, but you won't stay there."

The firm kept its promises: in the second month, I went from being a secretary general on the ground floor to a secretary in the mail room on the first floor, with a salary of 300,000 per month. The future was looking bright.

I quickly proved myself in the mail room. Speed, perseverance, lucidity, flawless letters: no one could have done better, and everyone benefitted. Within several weeks, I went from making 300,000 francs to 70,000 francs after the firm director personally told me in a meeting how satisfied he was with my work. He backed up this assertion by moving me to the third-floor writing room. I started as a copyist and very quickly became a lowly assistant. My tasks grew less and less complicated, the success of my career more and more assured, and I found my true calling as an employee when I pivoted from communications to popsicle sticks, sensitive work crucial to my new company's mission.

I was now pulling in 30,000 francs and, at the end of the month, after some scrimping, I could buy myself a school notebook in which I completed nightly exercises. My dream was to acquire a dip-pen with a wooden handle. I thought about it nonstop, but I had to let it go because the cost was far beyond my means.

I couldn't rise any higher in this organization short of perching myself on the roof, which was not permitted. At any rate, I had for several weeks been renting an apartment below street level to prevent any vertigo stemming from my rapid ascension. I was therefore greatly pleased when my living costs suddenly shot up, which decreased my salary to the subsistence level, which is to say, 12,000 francs. I had finally hit rock bottom. I moved out to live in a basement.

The popsicle sticks I was tasked with tracing became veritable marvels of discernment and precision. My employers kept citing me as an exemplar. One of my sheets was framed and subsequently purchased by the municipal museum. The most senior employees frequently came to me to ask for advice. I was held in such high esteem that my name had already twice been engraved in golden letters on a monument for the dead.

It was too good to last. Everything fell apart within a few hours. One morning, instead of drawing the required thirty-six sticks per line, I drew thirty-seven. With an awful screech, all business activity halted and, one second later, the firm ceased operations. The director acted honorably: after having dismissed me, he fired a 6.35 mm bullet into his right temple.

The future looked decidedly bleak.

But the past?

I'M NOW OUTSIDE THE DOOR of a very familiar apartment.

It's where I was born.

My parents, whom I believed to have died a long time ago, seem to still be living here. What state will I find them in? I pause before ringing the door.

My mother comes to let me in.

She hasn't changed. This is in fact my first mother on my granduncle's side, the one I was expecting. I see my sister near the door. She hasn't changed either and must be eight or nine. Needless to say, no one recognizes me.

"Come in," says my mother, who has surely taken me for a salesman or a missionary.

I enter and look around.

Nothing's changed. The giant lock still marks the boundary between the two living rooms and the bedrooms. The servant opens the sluice gates with the same peasant-like obstinacy she's always displayed. Slowly, the bedrooms sink below floor level and the living rooms appear.

The walls are lined with crushed birds, vulture skulls, and dead flesh oozing with mold. Giant eggs and deplumed wings hang from the ceiling, accompanied by the shrieking of birds of prey; the glass display case contains nests, tripes, and countless skeletons redolent of rancor and malevolence. I was unaware of the pact my father had made with these monstrous creatures; I realize it now: the pact of the rot collector. My father, so wise, so disinterested, dreamed of cramming the entirety of death into a cabinet. In the interest of science, he claimed.

All the rooms are filled with these larvae and detritus. Except the little parlor, which had remained a sandy desert into which no one ventured. It is there, perhaps, where come nightfall my father captures the birds that nourish his spirit.

"The Lord has sent you to us," my father murmurs upon seeing me. "Blessed be the Lord."

He doesn't recognize me, but I don't recognize him either. This must be another father. A brother, perhaps. Or a double. At any rate, a few moments later a second father, almost identical to the first, enters the room. I realize that the one I had taken for the elder father is in fact the younger father. And the fathers are already busying themselves and giving orders.

"Lunch is ready," says one. "We better head to the table."

"I set the table next to the desert-parlor," says the other. "I'm a little uneasy about it."

"Are you expecting an attack from that side?"

"I'm not sure. They'll definitely attack. And soon. But from where? From the desert, in theory. But they could also come from the hallway."

"We should have burned the furniture behind us. I'll double the guards. In any case, the desert is watched day and night. Keep your guns at the table, it's safer that way."

"It's ready!" my mother yells just then, so emphatically that the large crystal chandelier explodes.

The fathers, brothers, sister—who has split herself into twins—and the mother sit down. They point me to my place. First, we wash our feet. Then one of the fathers launches into a prayer thanking the Lord for our daily bread, which instantly fills the basket, while the water changes to wine, and above each of our heads shimmers the fleeting halo of an aureole. Next, we draw straws to determine who will be sacrificed first in the event of a shipwreck. Cautious as they are, the fathers hide their revolvers in their dishes, concealing them under enormous rations of soup. Every once in a while, I glance at the desert, but there's nothing on the horizon apart from the intermittent flashes from the constant atomic experiments taking place. Nothing suspicious stands out. There's sand, more sand, not even a clump of grass that one could mistake for an enemy. The fathers often look in this direction too. The children don't worry about it, and neither does the mother. She prepares the next day's soup as she eats, and she's knitting a wool sweater under the table with her feet. But the fathers are uneasy and make it known.

"I've got a bad feeling about today. We're entirely exposed here."

"We could have pulled the table back farther north."

"That wouldn't have changed anything. We'd have been better off building a mountain here."

"You can't be serious; it's crowded as it is."

"There's always space to be found. Or we also could have at least dug out a shelter under the floor.

"Maybe, yes. We should think about that. In any case, it would shield us from the heat."

It certainly is hot. The fathers are sweating so much into their soup that they end up finding it too salty. The mother, always on top of the situation, has sealed herself within a table mosquito net, behind which she appears like a famished ghost. The twins are not in sync: one is sweating while the other shivers from the cold. They're sisters with bivalent rather than unified responses. The brothers amuse themselves by drowning praying mantises in the soup tureen, which smokes like a volcano.

The peaceful meal is interrupted for several minutes by a violent sandstorm that descends upon the room without warning, wiping out everything in its path.

"Take cover," scream the fathers, their voices dissipated by the wind.

"I just dropped a stitch," says the mother as she dives under the table.

"Nasty weather for a meal, isn't it?" one of the fathers says to me as he spits out sand and several locusts.

"There'll be some sand biscuits for dessert now," notes the other.

"One man's desert is another's dessert," suggests one brother, drawing from his store of proverbs.

As for the other brother, he's taken advantage of the wind to fly a kite, which has effortlessly carried him off the ground and into the sky.

"Look at it go," one of the fathers remarks.

"Yep, he's done for," says the other father.

"I'm afraid so."

"All the same, maybe we can recover the kite?"

"Of course, but where?"

"When life gives you lemons, go fly a kite,"[3] declares the surviving brother, the fan of proverbs.

"I did tell him not to bring his kite to the table," murmurs the mother. "That'll teach him."

"He was raised poorly."

"He's raised himself just fine now."

"The fact is . . . I can't spot him anymore. If he ever falls from that height, he's going to get his new pants dirty."

All of sudden, the storm calms, and the mother rings the belfry bell to call the servant. Just as she arrives to clear the sand-filled dishes, a knight charges into the room at full tilt. The air fills with the steam from his steed's nostrils.

"Happy to see you," says the elder father. "Any troubling news?"

"None," the knight replies. "Nothing in the northern sector. I'm going to head southwest."

"Would you like some water?"

"No, thank you. My horse is currently drinking for us both."

"A little soup?"

"Thank you, but I'm fine. I ate up on the third floor. I see a storm came through?"

"And what a storm," says the elder father, hacking up a curtain.

"There was a veritable deluge on the fifth floor. Fortunately, my horse is waterproof."

"Be careful," warns the mother.

The knight sets off for the desert, where he soon vanishes, leaving a cloud of dust in his wake that momentarily blinds us before it falls and dissipates. The man is followed closely by a crew from Paramount, ready to film his exploits.

"A heroic age," the sister sighs.

"The horse ate all my soup," says one brother.

"A well-mannered child doesn't speak at the table," the mother tells him.

"Neither should a mother," the child responds.

The two fathers take no notice of this family banter. They check their weapons and suspiciously eye the chicken that has just been placed in the middle of the table.

"A chicken? Could it be a trap?"

"Unlikely," says the mother. "It's from the market."

"Which market?"

"The Wednesday covered market."

"Right. Well, as long as we're covered, there's no risk."

At this, the father lowers the gun he was holding on the suspicious chicken. Then, in several knife strokes, he carves the creature down to its skeleton, which he will showcase in one of the living room's cabinets.

"A gallinaceous chicken," he mutters as he retakes his seat. "I'd given up hope of ever finding one."

Meanwhile, one of the twin sisters, the elder-younger, is choking on a bone unfortunately lodged in a piece of white meat. She tries to cough it up in vain and dies a few seconds later, suffocated.

"The Lord gave her to us, and the Lord taketh her away," says one of the fathers in between bites. "Blessed be the Lord."

Suddenly, the Lord delivers a small miracle and resuscitates not the girl but the chicken, who pecks at some breadcrumbs, snags a fly from the air, and disappears.

"All that," sums up the younger father, "and we're back to square one. And I actually have to get going."

"Get going?" says the elder. "Then you won't be on watch this afternoon?"

"Unfortunately, no. I found a job."

"A job? That's odd. It's been years since you've had one. What is it?"

"It's a very simple enterprise. Its objective is to sell objectives."

"Objectives? To whom?"

"To other businesses. Those lacking them."

"But in theory, all businesses have an objective."

"Ours too, though it's not doing great. To tell the truth, we don't have a single client. But it all runs very smoothly."

"And the finances?"

"No problems there either."

"And what are you going to do for them?"

"Nothing."

"You'll get paid for doing nothing?"

"I never said I'd be paid."

"In that case, why would you go to work?"

"But no one ever shows up to work there."

"So this isn't what one would call a job, then?"

"A job, no. But employment? Yes."

"And where is this company located?"

"I've no idea. It doesn't have an address."

"Might as well say it doesn't exist."

"But of course it does, since I'm talking to you about it."

Mother busies herself around the conversing pair. She has finished knitting her sweater and is now unraveling it in order to purl it. She lets out a brief sigh and contemplates the fact that she's dedicated thirty years to this sweater, momentarily loses hope that she will ever finish it, then contentedly surveys the future, whose oblivion reassures her, and breaks into a vacant smile. My brothers and sister are amusing themselves as best they can. One opens his stomach to see if it's healthy, the other explains to his younger brother the essential regulations around prostitution, while the sister pours gunpowder into the matchbox her father will soon be reaching for.

Trifling amusements of a life that now strikes me as a bit antiquated, though not devoid of a certain charm. The servant arrives smiling with a cake, which the mother enthusiastically accepts, but the servant then suddenly collapses onto the middle of the table: an arrow has struck her in the back, a straight shot, fatal.

"An ambush," one of the fathers says as he crosses himself. "I knew the hallway was dangerous to cross at midday."

"This arrow didn't come from the hallway," says the other father as he signs the servant's death certificate. "Let's consider the matter carefully, especially the angle of the shot."

"What about it?"

"It's a ruse. This woman was not attacked. She shot herself in the back with an arrow."

"Why?"

"How should I know? Some kitchen-ache, perhaps? It's a culinary suicide, I'm telling you. And probably a trap. We'll have to keep our eyes open. But meanwhile, let's eat this cake; we'll deal with it later."

The mother slices up the whole cake with the aggressive strokes of a famished woman. A stream of blood spurts out, splattering one of the brothers, who collapses, succumbing to massive bloodstains.

"If this keeps up," says the mother, "we'll lose our large-family welfare."

No sooner had she spoken then rats start to pour out of the sliced cake and scurry off. They seem panicked and drunk on liberty.

"Rats flee a sinking cake," notes the brother.

The mother, forward-looking as she is, has caught a fleeing rat with her fork. She's already opening her mouth.

"It'd be better cooked with some pearl onions," says one father, the greater gourmet of the two.

"You might be right," says the mother as she drops the rat in the soup tureen. "While we wait, though, I could still eat something."

She casts a voracious glance at the remaining sister, pokes her arm with her fork, nods, and lets out a sigh.

"So skinny for her age."

Thus does the meal draw to a close.

The older father serves communion wine to the family members. He mists incense throughout the room and then thanks the Lord for all the blessings He's bestowed. Next, the children are sent to bury their brother, their sister, and the servant in the sand. The fathers get up, and the mother, her mouth full of sugared cloves, asks me if I enjoyed the meal. I hasten to reassure her.

"Will you be dining with us tonight?"

"Tonight is impossible. Perhaps another time."

"That's a shame. We're throwing a small party tonight. If, indeed, the fathers come back from their shift alive."

She smiles at me, a bit melancholic, with the profound resignation of women who have faced numerous disasters in their life. Then, her forlorn eyes suddenly widen, pupils dilating, and grow distressed and frantic.

"My keys," she murmurs, barely audible.

She searches around the room, overturns several objects, lifts up the tablecloth, which sends the dishes to the ground, rummages about, and heads back to me, half undressed.

"My keys," she's now screaming, "have you seen my keys?"

Within a few seconds, her consternation morphs into a raging madness. She falls down on her stomach, dives under the table, then a cabinet, gets back up and sends the cabinet through a glass door, nearly slits the remaining sister's throat to force a confession, breaks all the windows to see whether the keys have fallen onto the street, tears up several floorboards with a pickaxe, and rips open a wall that sounded hollow to her. She sweats, gasps, staggers, falls, gets back up and, pushed to her breaking point, now finds deliverance in a simpleton's psalmody, which she quietly hums.

"My keys . . . where did I put my keys? I had my keys, I no longer have my keys . . . Where are my keys?"

She had, incidentally, found them, and is holding them in her hand without realizing it. She no longer sees anything, hears anything, perceives anything. She hurries to the desert, falls on all fours in the sand, and sets off, stomach dragging on the ground, combing the sand with her nose and nails like a dog.

As for the fathers, they take little notice of this fit. They've seen others like it. They're currently using the large, overturned table as a barricade, positioned behind it with arms at the ready.

"Two o'clock," one of them states. "They may seize the opportunity."

"Unlikely. They'll probably wait until nightfall."

Is it two o'clock already? It's time for me to go to work. For a moment, I wonder whether I really need to take my leave from these two fathers. They haven't uttered one word to me and seem to inhabit a world wholly different from my own. However, to be courteous, I make my way over to them. I thank them and pay them my respects. They don't seem to hear me. I'm seized by a doubt and touch one of their arms: my fingers feel nothing but air. My suspicions were well founded: they had turned into mirages from living on the desert's doorstep. I leave them and return to the hallway.

There, a stranger approaches me. He has just come in through the small door at the end of the passage, the one leading to the kitchen.

"Ticket please."

I hesitate, but I must admit that decked out in his little ticket collector uniform, this man presents a very convincing picture of a train conductor.

"A ticket," I ask. "Why?"

"Why? For heaven's sake, are you kidding me? You're on a train and you're asking me why I need your ticket?"

A train? I see a window in the hallway covered by a curtain, which I pull aside. I note that we are indeed speeding through the countryside.

Forced to face the facts, I explain to the conductor that I must have boarded the train by mistake.

"By mistake . . . You board a train without thinking twice, as one would an airplane?"

"These things can happen."

"If you don't have a ticket, you have to get off."

I point out to him that the train is traveling quite fast.

"Take the first door on the left. The train's at the platform on that side."

At the exit gate, I'm asked for my ticket again. My circumstances are deemed suspicious, and I'm shunted off to the waiting room.

"Will I be here long?"

"It depends. Regardless, we won't be able to reach a decision until springtime."

What should I do while I wait? Lead a small, precarious life, perhaps? I pick one out and take it on as best I can. Each week I manage to drag myself along to Sunday, when I visit my local park.

It's nice out. Eucalyptus sequins fall everywhere, the drogozomes are in flower, and the poplucides are already losing their diamonds. Psilotruges apply makeup with their scraggly arms, scapelageous érogères lie in wait for passing bats to devour them in their arvicaves, and in the shadow of the parasitic scinthes, the catalpas whet the sharp fangs of their thousand dordènes.

I take a seat on a bench. Across from me, a woman is knitting three small red leaves that, once completed, she'll pin on the trees. A couple sits next to me. Somnambulant, weary, united in their mutual drabness, they exchange a few words, then go quiet and stare at the ground as if they'd been counting the stones on the path here for years and years.

A day goes by. The following day, at the same time, I see the knitting woman again. Then the couple.

"Nothing like a Sunday at the end of a workweek," says the man.

"They're necessary," says the woman.

"There's a nip in the air."

"It's that time of year."

This is exactly what they said yesterday. The next day, I see them again. They utter the same words, followed by silence. Nothing has changed, except that today, the man is wearing his wife's clothes, and she's wearing his.

I seek an explanation from the square's caretaker, an old, wounded veteran whose head, which was blown off by a cannonball, has been replaced by a hand.

"What day is it?" I ask.

"Sunday, of course," the caretaker answers.

"And yesterday?"

"Why, Sunday, naturally, just like tomorrow. You know very well that the square is closed during the week."

I should get out of here. It's easy, as the gates are open. I pass through them, but as soon as I'm out on the street, I collide with a woman who starts screaming, a crowd gathers, and a police officer scoops me up and deposits me in the square as if it were a jail cell. I've gathered that it's no use objecting.

The couple has just arrived.

"Nothing like a Sunday at the end of a workweek," says the man.

I take a seat as well. I unfold my newspaper. I start reading. Several months pass in this manner.

At the end of the fourth month, I finally get hungry. But I'm flat broke by now. Fortunately, the park's bank, which is located next to a cemetery reserved for caretakers killed in the line of duty at flower shows, hasn't yet closed. I open a bogus account of 4,000,453 francs. I sign over a check to myself for that amount. But they only give me 53 francs: in the wake of some metaphysical cataclysm, the number 4 has disappeared from civilization.

As one could easily imagine, this mishap has ripple effects. Mathematics, stripped of 4, has collapsed into orthography. The universe devolves into an infernal explosion of underhanded actions and immeasurably violent responses.

The repercussions, often hidden but no less harmful for that, are already being felt in the square. A series of unpredictable mishaps gradually snowball, carried forward by the stupendous power of the inexplicable, which is itself catapulted by the icy lightning bolt of the unforeseen.

The collapse of orthography seems to have infected syntax and grammar, because amid the muffled roar of the indefinite past, a shower of synonyms strikes at the heart of the gutturals, and a band of suffixes are already taking flight to plunge into ten centuries of conjugations. Seven irregular verbs have just penetrated botany, which, gnawed upon by an equation with twenty-three unknown variables, collapses into the fast-encroaching chaos. Yellow stems sprout forth at right angles to the hypotenuse, Jurassic corollas flower in the middle of a bed of possessive adjectives, blundering obtuse angles endeavor to analyze the future, plurals singularize themselves by adopting the pronominal mode, while the second declension, riding astride the principle of communicating vessels, suddenly erupts into the domain of administrative chemistry; this region explodes with a large flash of nothingness into the history of religions, carrying with it the critique of pure reason; geography abandons the core data of geology to seep into those of etiquette, and music theory tumbles like a screaming stone right into the core of civil law, after having shattered accounting to bits. The Holy Trinity falls back to Earth, abolished by gravity converted into thermometry; in the form of a six-footed electrode, the Father wails, the Son passes away with a musical note tinged with the gramoral, and the Holy Spirit is drawn toward absolute zero while spasmodically spitting out nitric acid. The universe's past arrives at high tide, bringing with it the principles of colonial digestion. Henceforth, silence clarifies the laws of perspective, the bacillus supplies electricity to Sino-Latin history, whose tall waves of eroticism discharge a flood of trigonometric progressions. The causal principle weighs no more than a liter of artificial respiration, the nervous system has plunged into metrics, rhetoric is buried under the acoustic, the debris from forty centuries of meditative hegemony is rotting under the proliferation of vegetation, and light, in an intense bout of reflection, finally discovers the principle of parliamentary monarchy.

A railway employee approaches.

"You weren't in here for too long, were you?" he asks.

"A year. It flies by. Especially Sundays."

"Excellent," he says to me. "We settled your case out of court. Here are your exit papers. I'm assigning you the number 993 and requesting simply that you return and check in every Thursday. To avoid any hassle, we had to register you as unclaimed lost luggage. That will allow you to be provisionally released with weekly monitoring. It is what it is. Those are the stipulations."

Yes, yes of course. It all makes perfect sense.

AND TODAY? What will happen today? Nothing much, I suspect. Nothing ever happens on a Monday.

Emerging from the warm, black cocoon of sleep, I pass into the pale cocoon of day. It's almost like moving from a world of down feathers to a realm of mud. I shiver as I dress, and feel like I'm putting on dead branches and trash.

Everything in the apartment is discolored this morning. A carpet of fog spreads across the floor. The carpet is covered in dew. The gas was cut off yesterday, the water three days ago. Water lilies spring up in the bathroom marshes, where a world of live cells, madregouses, prehistoric arnapa, and algae originating from the pipework's mysterious past germinate. Rats are dying of hunger.

There's no point in waking up my wife. She hasn't so much as glanced at me in weeks. She's stopped believing in my existence and is probably wondering why I even left, seeing as how I'm still here. Several days ago, I tried to impress her by returning from the office shirtless and tossing before her the corpse of a department head whom I had beaten to death while he was busy at work. She merely remarked that it didn't look edible. I haven't made a move since then.

What should I think about? I try to bathe and fail. It's not easy without water. I feel gray, porous, mineral. And the shard of glass I've been using as a razor has long since dulled. Luckily, I still have a stack of unpaid bills going back ten years. There's the gas bill that recently won a prize for the highest invoice in the capital, and also the direct taxes on indirect objects and local taxes on tax-free locales. I know that a bill never loses its value and that I could sell these to some collector. It's all about taking the time to find the right person. It's not possible today. I'm due at the office.

Who first thought of creating an office anyway? In short, somebody built one. Then another. Then millions, billions of others. They swallowed up towns, countries, inhabitants. I was deep in it now. Up to my neck. But how to escape? The office's exits merge into entryways, and every job leads to the office—as does every drain, emergency exit, panic attack—but the offices themselves lead nowhere.

Step by step, I make it to the metro.

"Chilly, isn't it?" says the ticket agent to me, the same words the ticket inspector tells me in passing.

Two seconds-in-command communicate across the platforms in Morse code using pennants. A new employee is learning how to get crushed between two train cars.

A train arrives. It's loaded with the same people as yesterday, seated in the same places. No one has moved. I usually sit in the front of the car, but today I remain standing so I can look out.

"Hey," a conductor says to me, "you think you're at the circus or something?"

I sit down.

When I arrive at the office, I do the same.

"Chilly, isn't it?" each employee says as they come in.

It's 9:05.

I open the folder of letters I have to answer. I panic: I only have ten letters to do today. Eight hours for ten letters, when I can easily do ten in an hour. I struggle in vain to restrain my hands as they pick up the company letterhead paper and slide it between the typewriter's rollers. They're already typing the opening words . . .

"Dear Monsieur, we have received your letter, and we are of the opinion that . . ."

I think. Thoughts sputter forth in a confused jumble. I reflect that for millions of years, algae and mollusks ruled the Earth, which was subsequently dominated by giant reptiles, until finally someone had the idea to create the company that employs me, and that this person was so proud of this achievement that he created the solar system. I think that we have no idea how nine planets and millions of asteroids sprang from this solar system, nor why we have to be born and then die, but that we do, however, know the detailed history of this company's founding. I think that the Earth spins around the Sun at a speed of 30 kilometers per second and that I'm here, anchored to this fireball speeding from one infinity to another, anchored to this desk, suspended in the void, while in my stoned, moronic, and oblivious state, earnestly affirm that we are sorry to learn that we have lost track of the package sent on the fourth and that we will do our utmost to remedy this mistake. I think that I'm speeding from my birth to my death at a rate of 100,000 kilometers per hour, that the Earth will spin on its axis for millions more years, that with any luck I myself will live for another thirty, that all of this has been definitively established, and that, despite everything, I'm sitting here at this desk, killing time at the rate of one syllable per second, without any hope of finishing it off for good, whereas time is killing me second by second and is guaranteed to finish me off.

For a moment, I deliberate between shouting and doing something. Though what should I do? Knock over an inkpot? Explode infinity? But there is an infinity of infinities in reserve. So what's the point? Best to close my eyes, let it drop, smile.

It's 9:10.

Reflecting on the creation of the universe, contemplating its destruction, plunging into an all-encompassing dizziness, and resigning myself to smiling all while composing a courteous letter: all that took just five minutes in the history of the world. It's hard to fathom. Already, my right hand has grabbed the day's second piece of correspondence, my left hand a piece of paper, my subordinate hand a carbon sheet, and the last a sheet of copy paper.

"Dear Messieurs . . . We were delighted to receive your letter of 34 December, and we sincerely believe that . . ." These words are communicated by the typewriter to my fingers, which immediately return the favor by sending them back through the machine. This typewriter, in sum, is ever so close to being able to function without me. It could probably manage just fine, but it has no desire to do so. It's deeply enmeshed in the conspiracy of clocks and electronic wires that regulate my personal journey. How am I to revolt against a machinery whose command center is invisible? I've just finished my second letter in two minutes. Wasted time; those minutes didn't count; it's still 9:10. And the head of the company has just walked in.

"Chilly, isn't it?" he tells us to make us think that his car, which comprises three rooms and a bathroom, isn't heated.

"The clock's fast," he remarks. And winds it back to nine o'clock.

I've thus managed to complete two letters in less than one second. The day looks promising. It's even exceeding all expectations, since at 9:15, a worker brings in a new clock. It reads 8:55. It stops at 9:20.

"It's the cold," declares a supervisor. Conscious of his supervisory responsibilities, he assures us that it must be much earlier, rehangs the clock, and adjusts the hands to 9:05.

"That'll be more accurate."

I'm on my eighth letter. How am I going to stretch the last two across 472 minutes? What should I do? Read aloud "Hail, Mary, mother of all industries," until I lose my voice? Or play alphabetic lotto with the typewriter keys? What about writing a hundred-page letter addressed not to a specific customer but to an Anonymous Client, to no purpose, to each and every client, to the nation and its dead, to God and his children, to a passerby, to whomever, to myself, to my yet-to-be conceived children, to the probable, to the possible, to the victor goes the spoils, to we're not asking for miracles, to the whole world? But this isn't possible. The typewriter, like the desk and the walls, belongs to the firm, and it can only type out numbers, commercial terms, icily courteous formulations, and information about sellers, salability, sales. The typewriter includes all twenty-six letters of the alphabet, but its repertoire is limited to certain combinations of phrases, always the same. The only remaining solution is to tap out polite formulations indefinitely. Or to think.

I give it a try. I look at the pencil lying on my desk. I sit still, focus, and think about it. I tell myself that it's a medium-sized pencil, sharpened, with no rough edges. Like a pencil, in sum. When you push it, it rolls. It rolls because it's cylindrical, and the cylinder is based on the notion of a circle. If I don't stop its momentum, it would fall off the desk. It looks like a rolling pin. But when you stand it upright, it looks like a tree trunk. A smooth and straight trunk. It also looks like a pencil. It is a pencil, of course. What does one do with a pencil? Pencil? Pencil what? Circles or crosshatches? Circles, preferably. They require more precision. But circles wear the point down faster. And I don't have anything handy to sharpen it. It's true that I don't use pencils often. Why do I have one? Doubtless because a real office must be stocked with pencils. I force myself to think more and more intensely about this pencil until I can't think anything more about it. The subject is exhausted.

But it's only 9:12.

The day advances. New bit players come and go. Business deals are devised, orders and counter-orders fly across the rooms. Phones ring, assistants bring in folders, others carry them out, emptied or fattened. Accessories are swapped, and all the sad little quotidian exchanges flutter about in a cacophony of phrases delivered as sententiously as so many court verdicts.

"It's important to remember to paste green stickers on the foreign post and red ones on the foreigners sent by post."

"From now on, you'll have to make fifty copies of your correspondence. Do you have enough carbon paper? And oxygen?"

"Don't forget to specify to our branches beyond the grave that should the temperature fall one degree, their reward points will be retroactively annulled."

"You have to redo the letter of 6/12. Replace 'Dear Sir' with 'Sir, dear Sir.' And add an 'etc.' That'll give it more oomph."

"Don't forget to spruce up the invoices sent to our mother company by the father of the brother of our sister company with some watercolor patterns."

"Attention: on the day after tomorrow you'll be receiving a letter addressed to us in error. Please tear it up, glue the pieces back together, and send it back to us after placing it in an envelope the wrong way up."

"For the hundredth time, Mademoiselle, I'm telling you that it's impossible to write a decent letter when you're not wearing a bra."

"You're telling me you never use the circumflex in your correspondence? Reading your letters, one would think you have something against proper writing style."

A slew of orders slowly descends upon us, and a few even reach my desk, but discolored, crumpled, as if they've traversed kilometers of compressor pipes. I never listen or object to any order. I'm informed of certain decisions because regulations require it, but everyone knows it's just a formality and a complete waste of time. They've been waiting on an urgent report from me for two years now. Sometimes they make a bit of a stink, but without conviction. Work counts for almost nothing here; only one's presence matters. And yet, even if no one showed up at the office, business would keep humming along in the silence, propelled by the forces of inertia and ennui, and millions of profits would continue to pour into the banks' filthy coffers.

I look around and listen. The air's been sucked out of the room, as if the ennui has become tangible, a new-spun material invisible to the eye. I have the sensation of being caged within a day that risks extending beyond the entirety of my past and future. A day without definite end in which, to return home, be it tonight or in a century, I'll simply have to board the last hearse. My coworkers, however, seem to be experiencing a normal day, one in which seconds and minutes ultimately roll into hours. I alone am outside of time. For a moment, this realization knocks the wind out of me, and I look at the clock for reassurance. I'm at a loss: 9:13.

Could this merely be an error? The office clock isn't infallible. I pick up the phone and call the time. There's no answer: just someone snoring.

I've come to accept that for one reason or another, I'm condemned to hover between 9:00 and 9:15. But then what about the others? After all, we're sharing the same space. I view them, they view me, we give each other the *vous*. To verify my suspicions, I get up, borrow an eraser from a recently hired secretary; she smiles in response to the formal smile I give her. If her smile, which exists in a time different from mine, reaches me in spite of everything, then the relationship between time and space must be distorted.

What time could it be for the others? Probably around noon, as their accelerated rhythms indicate that a break is near. Some employees are already moving into new roles. Does this mean several years have passed? The facts back me up: someone whom I saw enter as a warehouse worker in the morning is now editor-in-chief and is giving me orders. And moreover, he's now sporting a beard. And a wedding ring. People discuss projects with me that I've never heard of, and we're deftly managing branch offices unknown to me.

"Are you nuts?" says a department head to me. "You're answering a letter from two years ago?"

And now everything around me, which seems at once familiar and distant, foreign, gradually fills out, becomes the world's stage, the theater of events. The office, however, remains apart, isolated, like a pocket of calm amid an inferno of mishaps. An inferno? You can say that again. The company's ground floor appears to be going up in flames. The fire travels up to the second floor, then the third. We're on the sixth, and panic is setting in. The manager comes out of his office, furious.

"What's the big deal?" he says. "Back to work! Where do you think you are? There's a fire . . . I get it. But that's no reason to goof off."

The fire has in fact consumed the entire building, from the basement to the ninth floor, but the office has been spared. The whole neighborhood has collapsed, the office alone having escaped the cataclysm. Next, a tornado sweeps through and carries the room all the way to the western plains, after which an extremely powerful flood deposits it right in the middle of another city. The office survives amid the floods, tides, and cyclones. And still nothing happens. It's 9:20, and I'm given an urgent letter to write immediately. The world, meanwhile, seems to be ending, and the entire city is slowly sinking into the water-soaked, eroded ground. The office alone floats along like a raft, and the managers order us to close the windows to keep out the drafts. A volcano awakens, a mountain chain coughs up the Earth's entrails, an ocean dries out while another spills over and topples two now useless continents, and the office falls into a bottomless crevice between two shattering glaciers, then reappears on the other side of the Earth, with no damage or casualties.

"Please, Mademoiselle," says a secretary to a typist working on the ceiling with her head hanging down and her skirt riding up. "Your thighs are on display and distracting the workers. Come back down to the floor immediately."

It appears that giant lizards have invaded the city, earthquakes are breaking out in the suburbs, the whole downtown is burning in a sea of oil that's broken through the dams, and the Earth is now but a chaos of ravaged landscapes.

"What with all the commotion, my inkpot tipped over," an officemate informs me.

World war is declared, and the bomber squadrons are already doing low-altitude surveillance runs over the city. Some fly by the office, in one window and out another, the roar of a civilization at its peak. Unfortunately, the office has remained neutral, and is recognized as such by the Red Cross. So there's definitely no exit. Stupefied by boredom, I think of crossing the border in spite of everything. I'm going to plead illness and head out into the city when I see that they're getting ready to shoot an employee against the big wall in back.

"Can you imagine?" someone says to me. "He wanted to enlist and desert the office. Now when we're drowning in orders."

What can I do? Take up another letter.

"Dear Messieurs, it was with keen interest that we learned of . . ."

And my interest grows so keen, so strong, that little by little I feel myself waver. One more second and I'll collapse. I fall down. But I seem to realize that this is not sleep. It's not death either, nor is it a loss of consciousness or a fainting spell. A wormhole, that's what it must be. That I was unable to proceed past 9:30, even though it must be at least 11:00, ultimately caused my temporal state to collide with my living state, which was proceeding apace, to carve out a depression all the deeper for being invisible.

Fortunately, a little accident occurs just then.

A bomb falls through the roof and explodes in the office. It's a timebomb. Stunned, I note that I, like everyone else, am unharmed. The clock reads 6:30.

The day is over.

I can start a new one all over again.

BUT WHAT'S THE USE?

These days ... Always matinees in the morning. Soirees at night.

And then these identical-looking doors ...

In any case, I'm unable to see a door without knocking on it. That very morning, I enter a luxurious office that could only belong to a CEO.

"You wished to speak with me?" asks a CEO, in fact. "I'm right here. What would you like?"

I'm moved by this solicitude, but I first have to work out just what kind of CEO I'm dealing with. Feeling a bit anxious, I leave the office to gather information. I'm informed that I'm at an insurance company. I make sure I have this right at the info desk, then head back into the CEO's office.

"So, what would you like?" repeats the CEO.

But already distracted by his work obligations, he loses his train of thought, opens a small closet door and disappears behind it, emerges re-outfitted in a three-piece wool suit, verifies the water level and temperature of his safe, signs two checks and his death warrant, schedules a couple meetings, cancels the piano delivery man, hires a strong-arming goon to be his right-hand man, deposits his cigar in the ashtray, and asks me to follow him after swapping out the portrait of the company founder on the wall with a sign that reads "No spitting." He walks through several offices handing out oranges to the staff, issues a big family speech about the wonderful work the team is doing, cleans a fingernail, suddenly notices me, and begins shouting.

"So, you wanted to speak with me?"

Just that moment, he spies himself in a mirror, primps, quickly realizes he's made things worse, and says as much. Vexed, he takes the door, resells it for six times its cost, starts a currency-exporting operation from the profits, finds a job for "Better late than never" at the Society of Nonagenarian Inheritors, a position for "A good name is better than gold" in the Matrimonial Association of Judo Maids, and a spot for "There's more than one fish in the sea" in the Little Sisters of the Gilded Virtues. He notes that his revenue curve is shooting upward, that it's smashing through the ceiling and turning into a lightning rod, then a space rocket. He capitalizes by slashing salaries 20 percent and requiring August to count as two months with night shifts thrown in, sets an example by shooting one of the pillars of the company without warning, sees it collapse in a cloud of dust and rubble, then finds himself sitting on the sidewalk, his clothes in tatters. He sells the ruins of his company for a bite of bread, then trades that to a tramp for a single shoe, swaps the sole for a pencil, the shoelaces for an old notebook, the heel for an idea for a novel, which he only has to write, writes it, and receives a substantial advance from an editor that allows him to buy a grocery store-bookshop.

Not wishing to distract him from his new business venture, I decide to come back later. It's nice outside, and a voyage to the tropics is just what I need. So I return home, leave a couple of hundred-franc bills for Mygale, and take my biggest sailboat out of the garage. As there is only a light breeze, I row across the capital. I travel up the grand industrial canal to reach the nearest stream and, following it to its source, hang a right to the sea, then turn off to the less trafficked ocean, that of the southern banlieue. At the first port stop, I stow a cargo of plump women whom I keep fresh in salt and ice. And the ship sails on to a bright future. The sun beats down, even at night. The sea is calm, and when it gets choppy, I give it some bromide. I sail along as if in a dream until the day the sailboat, buffeted by winds on all sides, misses a tack and takes a good chunk from the outermost cape of a freshly restored continent. The damages are substantial and the fine, which was already exorbitant in francs, is levied in dollars. Even by renting an unassuming storefront from which to sell my sailboat, I'm sunk. I have to look for work.

I took a job at a funeral parlor. For my first burial, I had the idea of conducting it at breakneck pace, to the frantic rhythm of the galloping horses of the Old West, hoping thereby to mitigate the traditional gloominess of the ceremony. This decision led to numerous headaches, as well as monthly damages to be paid to the deceased's family. Haunted by my ever-growing debt, I worked even harder. As a conductor on a subway train, I delayed us for hours at each station because I took it upon myself to personally check that each rider was comfortably settled and satisfied with our service. Yet again, my actions led to my dismissal, not to mention the fines, with interest, that management slapped on me.

I didn't let myself get discouraged. I washed up in a shipping department and was back up on my feet in no time. For three days, I didn't take a single break and made so much progress that I had not only completed the tasks of all the company's employees but also all their work going forward two years. Management no longer had any choice but to fire me, along with the rest of the staff.

They also demanded that I cover the entirety of the unpaid salaries for the following three years, on top of 22 million in psychological damages.

Seeing no other solution, I wrote a check covering all my debts. I was told that my account definitely lacked sufficient funds to cover it. I immediately alerted the soup kitchen, which handled the matter, and no one mentioned it again.

"Is that you?" asks the CEO of the insurance company upon my return. "I looked all over for you. You wanted to talk to me, if I recall. One minute and I'm all yours."

He's already long gone.

Seized by a sudden panic, he announces a period of austerity, dismisses an employee, cuts another one in half, gets to work himself, starts to write a speech in pencil, pivots to a public appeal, then dictates a prose poem for the unveiling of a work table, cancels an order for vises, delivers two pieces of advice on vice, revises his plan, and devises a series of devices. Suddenly spent, he notices my presence.

"You again?" he says to me. "You've come at an awful time, right during the summer holiday."

Indeed, sitting in the shade of their typewriters, typists are sunning their exposed thighs in the neon lights. One particular secretary, wrapped in a form-fitting bathing suit in the front of the office, goes to change behind a chair in the waiting room. Some shirtless employees are playing ball and making sly business innuendos. A young editor has just bought a sandcastle and, shovel in hand, waits for high tide. Others are running in place with towels across their backs, soaking wet, teeth chattering, doing some filing to stay warm. Even the old accountants, who have long been stumbling about in the labyrinth of an ancient invoice, treat themselves to footbaths.

All this reminds me that I promised to call a young woman whose name and address I've completely forgotten. The boss appears surprised when I ask him for permission to use his telephone.

"The telephone, you say? And what exactly is that?"

I explain it to him. Straight away, he summons a manager, whom he proceeds to berate.

"How do you expect this business to function if we don't even have a telephone? Initiative, my dear fellow, that's what's lacking. I'm sorry, but this time I'm going to crack the whip. At the stroke of noon, we're going to put you out on the street in a boat outfitted with oars and provisions for three days. That'll teach you a lesson. And make sure that we immediately install this . . . how do you call it . . . this telephone? Who's free to work on this right now?"

"I'm not really sure. As you're aware, we just took an inventory of typos with a view toward reassigning our lower-level staff."

"I don't give a damn. Do you have the accountant-zinc worker on hand?"

"Not currently. He's busy sending out free bonus vouchers backdated after the purchase of the seventh item less three non-refundables."

"And the team of microfiche embroiderers?

"On maternity leave."

"And the busters of balls?

"At a conference."

"Unbelievable. Is everyone in this company hard at work? Are you serious? And the agronomic inveiglers?"

"It's Thursday. Their religion . . ."

"They should change their religion for starters! Come to think of it, we'll formally ban the practice of religion companywide. From now on, I don't want it mentioned. Send out a memo. While you're at it, set up a meeting about the planisphere for tonight at six. And what happened to my geologic map of the offices, with the different strata of documents buried underneath? You were supposed to send that to me ten days ago. Take down this urgent letter. Are you there? I'll dictate it to you tomorrow. But still send it by end of day through the pneumatic. And where are the smokers this morning? What does the nocturnal barometer read? I noticed yesterday that someone left a door closed in one of the offices. I don't want to see that happening anymore. And the floors, when will we finally have one on the fourth floor? We can't work forever in thin air at that height. Such negligence in this operation! I have to think of everything. So you don't have anyone who can install . . . what is it again? . . . this telephone? Your deputy, for instance?"

"Impossible, he's on the phone."

"He's on the phone? Where?"

"Somewhere in the building, I suppose."

"But that means we do have one, a telephone. You really should have told me right away, for god's sake."

Having quickly regained his composure, he turns to me, more agreeable than ever.

"Would you please follow me, sir?"

I enter a phone booth and dial the number of the young woman I'd promised to call. I must have misdialed, because I've never heard this ringtone before. It seems to be ringing in a giant abandoned mansion. No one picks up, but I can't help but stay on the line, hypnotized by that icy wave vibrating in the void. Finally, someone or something picks up the receiver. And then I hear the laugh, a mirthless, purposeless laugh, thin, dry, monstrous.

Overcome with terror, I redial the number. This time, only the ringtone answers. Putting on a bold front, I ask what's new, then whether it would like to go on a date sometime this week.

"Busy," it replies, incessantly.

I try a new approach, and I soon find myself carrying on various conversations at the same time.

"Hello? Police? I'm alerting you that I was murdered at dawn. My corpse is still at home. You won't have trouble recognizing me. I'm the only one in the room."

"Excellent. Take this down. You'll drop off a liter of you know what to me at you know where. And don't forget to wipe off your fingerprints."

"Attention, we're preparing to land. Descend to three meters. We're flying over the grand salon right now and the chimney. The dresser is in view, prepare the dining room table for landing. Clear a path and remove all the pottery."

"I've just looked over your file, Madame. We processed your order, and your package left our office twelve years ago now. We request your patience for just a few more days. The post office is currently experiencing delays in delivery."

I'm about to hang up when a voice addresses me.

"Is that you? And it's only this year that you deign to let us know you won't be coming into work? Don't bother showing up tomorrow. You're done here, got it?"

"What happened? I looked for you everywhere but couldn't find you. I did after all tell you to show up waving a red pennant . . ."

"What is it? I've been trying to get you on the phone for three years now. I haven't even eaten for fear of missing your call. What, did you want to starve me to death?"

Feeling a wave of nausea coming over me, I leave the phone booth and notice that there's water up to my waist. Everything is now underwater. All the equipment and furniture has drifted off, carried along by a strong current that's already worn away the partitions. The company must have been liquidated for some reason or another. The current is quite dangerous. Even the pencils and corks are sinking to the bottom. I have to grab onto a door, dodging the filing cabinets rushing past me like tree trunks.

Luckily, I meet an employee in the hallway traveling upstream in his canoe. He hauls me on board and we reach the executive suite after avoiding an eddy around the main staircase. Up here, the offices are like little inlets where it's easier to navigate. The water is very clear, and one can plainly distinguish every flourish of the carpet's pattern, whose flowers are morphing into algae and anemones. The CEO is still at his post, very dignified as he sits in water up to his chin.

"You really have terrible timing," he tells me. "I've sunk my business."

Indeed, the water has, little by little, reached the ceiling. It's becoming difficult to get around. Employees and managers are working in slow motion; salesfish either follow in their wake or speed around them.

"Care for a cigarette?" asks one manager, holding out a packet that turns into a shapeless mass and soon disintegrates.

"Mademoiselle," he asks a young woman paddling her arms and legs weakly as she passes over the table, "would you be so kind as to change the water in this vase?"

The young woman gracefully spins around overhead, momentarily assumes the pose of a dead leaf, then a winged waterlily, doubles over, and in one uninterrupted unfolding, displays to us the mind-blowing vision of her two thighs as they slowly open and close beneath a dress that seems to be breathing like an enormous mouth of fabric.

I call her over. She approaches me, trailing bubbles.

She is opal and flowing, smooth and snow white. I ask her name.

"Solène," she replies.

"That's not an office name."

"It's my name nonetheless."

"And what do you do here?"

"I smile. I was hired to smile."

She certainly has the most extraordinary smile imaginable. It's a smile without any flaws, no trace of the morbid or unwholesome, no coquettishness. A smile that can peel open the world like an orange. A smile that electrifies like the invention of the lightbulb, that rings out like the treble of a hi-fi speaker. She takes my hand. I'm taken aback by such gentleness. But what can I say? How could I resist her?

"The water's wonderful, you know?" she says. "Would you like to have dinner with me tonight?"

"Tonight? So soon?"

"I'm asking you out, yes."

"But why?"

"Because I enjoy spending time with you. We'll have a great time tonight. The whole evening is ahead of us."

"A whole night . . ."

She smiles again.

"I really can't stay up too late. I have to get up at eleven tomorrow morning."

"We'll actually be going to bed very early. And where will that be? Your place or mine?"

"You at your place, and me at mine. It's better that way, I promise. I like talking to you so much. You're wonderful, you know that?"

Thus do the minutes, our pleasantries, and my hopes come and go. I try to convey my desire to Solène, but in vain. She strides through my innuendos as if they were clouds of smoke.

"Who exactly are you?" I ask her.

"A glass of water."

"Can I take a sip then?"

"If you drink me, you'll no longer be able to see me."

I accept defeat. I can't resist staring at her, watching her. We exchange telephone numbers. Then she casts a worried look at the ceiling.

"It's getting colder," she tells me. "I'm going to get dressed."

The wind is in fact picking up.

Soon, it's blowing everywhere, throwing open cabinets, doors, windows, whipping up reams of paper in its trail.

The water has receded completely within minutes, swept away by the breeze. The fish, now all dried out, are left hanging in the air. Some are struggling. Others are decalcifying on the floor. Still others are already strung up from the ceiling, smoked.

"What a day," says the CEO.

He straightens up, looks around, and doesn't seem to recognize the place, littered as it is with junk.

"What am I doing here?" he asks me.

He notices a call button and presses it with his finger. The air in the room grows heavy, becomes a deep green, with a hint of blue, an almost tangible color. The least movement produces a flurry of sparks that crackle and spew forth purple gleams.

The CEO then turns on the lights. A constant whistling can be heard, after which a strong odor of gas floods the room. Resigned, he lights a cigarette, which causes a smaller explosion than one would have imagined.

"You wanted to speak with me, I believe? I'm listening. How can I help you?"

On a whim, I tell him that I'd like to shoot a movie.

"A movie? Excellent idea. You'll begin tomorrow at 9:00 a.m. sharp. Stop by accounting and set yourself up with a 27 million advance."

Things can be so simple sometimes.

My first film, which ran to one hour, was devoted to the color gray, the only concessions being the occasional tonal change. At certain points, the background music, which consisted of two guitar notes, emphasized the imperceptible transition between tonalities.

For my second film, I wanted to make an epic work. It would have a running time of six days and six nights and completely ruin the production company that picked it up.

In a stroke of bad luck, I realized after wrapping up shooting that I had remained in the movie. And getting out wasn't so simple, as I had been relegated to a sparsely populated scene on a set with no props: I would never be able to find a telephone or even a sheet of paper to request help.

I had to resign myself to walking from room to room and, as my role was so small, I wasn't able to inhabit any consciousness whatsoever, anything resembling a fleshed-out character, during the film's six-day runtime. Even in my one scene, in which I played the role of a chance passerby, I could barely be said to exist, and then only vaguely. Smartly dressed in a dark suit, I sauntered among the unavoidable pitfalls of a jungle. Approaching a tree, I suddenly encountered a presumably lost explorer crawling flat on his stomach, bleeding, wounded, pale, and half dead.

"You wouldn't have the time, would you?" this wreck of a man asked me.

Indifferent, I replied that I was sorry and marched on.

That was the end of my part, as the camera soon swung back to the injured explorer. He was the scene's star. Luckily, my lines weren't hard to deliver, and during those several minutes of existence once every six days, I had the leisure to think of a means of escape. Should I descend from the scene and into the movie theater? Impossible, already tried it. What about leaving through the backstage? There wasn't any—the movie was shot in a real jungle. If my scene was in a street or an apartment, I would surely have located a door. But in a jungle?

I DIDN'T GET OUT UNTIL 37.

One evening, instead of walking by the injured man, I decided to stay still. This was quite grueling: fifty years of cinematographic technology were reeling me forward. Mustering all my determination, I focused on one thing: not moving. With a violent tear I thought would destroy me, I managed to rip myself out of the filmstrip, which I saw spinning away on its path to glory and posterity, leaving me behind standing in place.

And now here I was in the jungle again, with no movie, no injured explorer, no set. But I was still in a dark suit and sporting gloves, a cane, and a bowler hat. Dressed like this, I couldn't possibly make a bad impression were I to come across a relative or a financial backer.

It was hot, but the bowler hat afforded me some protection. However, not having a watch bothered me. If I could have foreseen this circumstance, I would have slightly modified the script. But no matter. It was never too late to envisage a brighter future.

The light filtering through the tree branches is in fact coming from a tropical sun. An invisible sun in a sky shielded from view. Nothing but enormous leaves, roots, swollen bulbs, opulent flowers yawning with boredom in their thorny lairs, profuse vegetation and its dyspeptic eruptions, overflowing with fat and rot, sap and humidity.

The silence.

I decide to forge ahead. Ideally, I'd find a well-shaded path that would lead me to a town as quickly as possible. I'd really like to catch a movie tonight. And anyhow, my shoes are getting soaked, and my shoelaces are on the verge of fraying completely. I find all of this quite irritating.

I come to a clearing and note that there are two suns in the sky. That's why it's so hot. I've been walking a good three hours and not one sign of animal life. Not even a carnivorous plant. Even the quicksand seems lethargic and in a bad state. How did I manage to shoot a tragic scene in such a lifeless jungle?

Oppressed by this inertia, I'm aimlessly wandering when a strident voice suddenly rings out. Given its reach, the voice seems to come from on high, transfixing the entire landscape with its awesome resonance.

What's more, this voice speaks.

"On the fifth floor, ladies and gentlemen," says the voice, "you'll find our lingerie section. To browse it is to buy it; to buy it is to love it."

This anonymous voice reminds me of something. I can't possibly deny that I'm in a jungle, but it's equally impossible to deny that this honeyed voice, servile and dictatorial, is coming from a department store loudspeaker. I hesitate for a moment, trying to locate the elevator that should take me to the fifth floor, then I set off. The voice continues its dulcet solicitations, insinuating, coolly welcoming:

"Why wait? Everything here was designed expressly to be purchased by you. Do you think that even one of these thousands of ribbons or buttons was conceived, drawn up, painted, and produced in vain? Wrong. There's a client for each variety. And your presence here proves it."

This monologue grabs my attention, of course, but even as it demonstrates that commerce always reigns supreme, it doesn't strike me as convincing. First off, I don't need anything, and furthermore, I see nothing to buy. I can't help but find this marketing a bit out of place here. The voice is no less confident for it, just as emphatic in this green emptiness as if it were addressing a gathered crowd.

"Fate has served you well to lead you here, and now it's our turn to serve you. Our elevator cables snap only once a year, and according to your horoscope, today's your lucky day. Did you have any idea? Our cash registers can swallow up ten million in a single second and sing a thank-you message to you after each transaction. In the death department, check out our display of fatal accidents and a retrospective of pastry sculptures depicting twelve famous disasters. A dead person who comes our way can rest assured. On special offer this week: a toothpaste that will leave your corpse with a dazzling smile."

Where have I heard this voice before?

"Did you know about our dissection services, which are always at your disposal? Know thyself better, get dissected. What's there to lose? Absolutely nothing. Because in a one-time offer this week only, we're giving out free eternal life vouchers in our missals and calvary department. Currently on sale: rubber crucifixes for the bathroom, sparkling mass wine, charitable cashboxes specially designed for checks made out to cash, and soon the *Saint Père* himself, disguised as Saint Nick, will appear to let the gifts from little children come to him."

I move forward. The voice follows me. The whole world is hers. Where could it be coming from? From the sky, it would seem.

Could I be nearing the kingdom of God? In any case, business seems to be booming up there.

Something has just happened. An obvious sign of civilization rises to the surface: emerging from a clump of vegetation, a traffic light appears before me. I walk past it. Then, an undercover cop emerges from a neighboring marsh.

"Apparently, you didn't notice the red light? I'm sorry, but I'm going to have to report you."

Without letting me gather myself, he reels off fourteen of the most difficult irregular verbs in the subjunctive for me in one breath. Only then does he let me go. As for the voice, it's still following me. It's always there, I can feel it, even when it's silent. This must be the prologue to something.

"Gentlemen, why linger empty-handed? Our hunting and murder department awaits. Once you pick up one of our factory-made rifles, you'll be heading off to war to try it out in no time. That's the spirit, sir, nice shot! Right between the eyes? Congratulations! And you hit a manager to boot? Take the machine gun then, that'll speed things along. One model stands above the rest: the bivalent 'Slayer,' with a jumping tripod that allows for the maximum possible dispersion. Take advantage of this exceptional opportunity: you can't make up for lost bullets."

This scene finally stirs up a tangible memory for me. I must, therefore, have worked in this department store and stood under this sonorous shower. And the voice is seeking me out: without a shadow of a doubt, it wants to reclaim me.

"Speak any syllable on a trial basis, no matter which, and the square root of the indicated item will immediately be given to you, with the bill attached to the other side."

Help!

But how could I flee from a voice? How escape from a jungle in which one is lost?

"Anything at all at whatever the price, that's our motto. Picture it and it'll be yours. And don't forget our rewards program—in which you can enroll willingly or by force—as well as our favorable commission rates for armed shoppers. Have you considered spending your paycheck? Rest assured, we'll handle it for you. This month, from the 18th to the 5th, there's a spectacular price hike on all discounted dreams, and you can trade in your intimate sorrows for wholesale value. Next month we're leasing out revolutionary holidays at a discount. And within the next few days, there'll be a major retrospective on yet-to-be-invented objects. It's all coming soon, right here."

There's a definite shift in the landscape. Amid a thick pile of leaves, I make out a rack, empty, covered in moss, but a store rack nonetheless. The voice is so skilled in the art of persuasion that it probably managed to conjure up the furnishings.

I hear the distinct staccato chant of cash registers belching out their rapacious beeps. I can already make out certain conversations from within the green abyss. It's disquieting, because I can't see any shoppers or salespeople at the moment. Fifteen minutes later, however, I meet a gardener walking between the trees and watering the roots of these mummified grotesques with care. Soon, though, the product posters, neon tubes, price tags, and baubles stage their assault on nature, which retreats. Devoured by commodities. The scene still explodes with overgrown green vegetation, but the metal and glass, the nylon and plywood, are taking root, invading, imposing themselves. The rays of a gleaming housewares extravaganza are already filtering down through the branches above. Shoppers and salespeople emerge from the bog. Moving forward becomes harder and harder. Apart from the upholstery fabric, the pale vines, and the spaghetti creeping down from the treetops, various objects rise up from the mud to block my path: trestle tables, with products arranged on them in pyramids; mirrors and false doors; moss curtains; piles of laundry soaking in puddles of moldy water; not to mention the shoppers, who are becoming more and more frenzied, muddy, and covered in thorns and twigs but hardly concerned with their appearance, so fixated are they on their desired objects.

At this point there's almost no greenery left, and the little slice of nature that does remain has been repainted yellow or red. The jungle is fading away, growing flat and stunted and then disguised, remade anew, as the scene is coated in soap, varnish, and snowy detergent that make the surfaces sparkle. Ceilings crush the trees, which collapse into something like circus tents supported by wax angels. The ponds and puddles dry up, the ground morphs into a linoleum surface decorated with the store logo. Rugs materialize, glass displays shine, pylons rise up like elevators. Doors open and snatch up customers, who are dragged into an unknown universe and launched into the beating heart of commerce.

Soon the jungle is but a thing of the past. The odd vestige is still visible: a branch here, a leaf hanging off a mannequin, a root emerging from a cream puff, a glimpse of scorching sky peeking through two meat stalls, the swamp bubbling up between two floorboards.

All of a sudden, that sound of a waterfall.

I hesitate. Will the jungle reassert itself by unleashing an infernal swarm of snakes feasted on by millions of carnivorous insects? Or will a flood carry off the store until it plummets several hundred meters down? That looks to be the case, because I approach the edge of a chasm. And I see it all before me.

I'm on the seventh floor of the store.

I wait, motionless. I watch the shoppers enter, pushed forward by other customers, determined, aggressive, rapacious. Moving like supercharged tornados, they are sucked in through doors, spit out of elevators, or expelled down the stairs, cutting a path through ramparts of glittering merchandise, passing between the luxury earthenware and the laughing toothbrushes to rush into an aquarium and emerge as toilet brushes, then proceeding to disembowel several ditherers and plunge headlong into the lingerie section, pausing for one second to choose between the Mother's Day department and the Discovery Palace, another second for their underwear to slide all the way down to the slippers, after which they carry on with muffled steps to the register, which returns their money while they return the favor by heading to the fifth floor, stripped bare but content, and walk with open mouths through a liver pâté tunnel before getting into position to perform the quadrille of the famished, then plodding on to another register, which sends them off on an escalator, the so-called rolling staircase, rolling along and on a roll as they roll up on some children's trumpets, that makes 200 plus one duck for the bathtub and a bathtub for the duck, let's say 400,000 for now, shattering the price ceiling, whose collapse buries alive 300 customers, which is of no consequence considering our pharmacy extravaganza will gladly get you back on your feet, or into a coffin, always as you wish, always at your service . . .

Before me, a gate opens with a metallic clatter. Are they going to free me? A young woman in uniform brushes against me with her breasts, which, incidentally, are registered.

"Going down, sir?"

The gates of the elevator close me in. The floors whiz by.

The gates open. I'm ejected.

I STROLL THROUGH the food department, where all the colors and sounds are washed out by the foul odor of an overstuffed stomach, and stop in front of a butcher's stand to speak to a saleswoman.

"The exit?" I ask. "How does one get out of here?"

She looks at me with a touch of concern bordering on pity.

"You have a toothache, don't you?" she asks me.

Toothache? How does she know? I do in fact have a toothache. Now that I think about it, I feel something behind my face. Or rather, I feel as if my face has a reverse side, a backstage. A misshapen rodent is fiercely digging a burrow into my gums.

"The doctor will see you in just a moment," she tells me after consulting her order book.

She returns several minutes later, still dressed in white, but splattered in blood from head to toe.

"Please come in," she says, opening a door.

This dental office is so drained of life that I can barely tolerate looking around. Suspended from very high on the ceiling are the jawbones of the dentist's clients. Some are still glistening. The others have decalcified.

"Have a seat," a man's voice says to me.

I obey and settle into a chair with various controls and straps. The chair tilts back, elevates, and lightly sways, then stops moving as two straps grip my wrists.

"Shall we begin?" the voice says to me.

There's no one in front of me. No one behind me. Suddenly, I see an eye. It's an electric eye, gleaming, bright red, the eye of the machine fixed to the ground to the right of the chair. This is the machine that is speaking and will perform the surgery. In fact, it's coming toward me, and emerging from its innards are a small mirror, a steel bracket, and two tiny scalers that bob up and down as they trace a circular path toward my mouth.

"This won't do at all," says the machine. "Open your mouth, please."

The mirror and the bracket pry open my mouth. Other instruments emerge from the machine's gullet: cotton gauze, scissors, and a high-speed drill that starts spinning. The eye has turned green.

"Ah, I see," says the machine. "It's less serious than I feared. Another face seems to have sprouted in your aching tooth. I think I can make out the eyes. A little zap of the laser and it should be gone forever."

A scream that is completely alien to me erupts from deep within my face, after which the machine immediately deposits a wad of cotton gauze in my mouth. It's suffocating me, and I try to alert the machine. But it's deaf to my cries, and I'm growing mute. I'm suffocating. Luckily, I'm expanding at the same time. The cotton is refashioning me. I'm turning into a wad of cotton gauze. I soon burst open into a great expanse of wadding. I've disintegrated and already been reassembled; my hands themselves have become mere packets of gauze.

"Have you come to a decision?" the saleslady asks. "You've been fiddling with the absorbent cotton for fifteen minutes now."

The thing is, in the last few seconds, the voice on the loudspeaker has ceased for the first time, as has the music. The store's six levels now look like one undifferentiated block with no definite purpose, which thousands of mice swarm over as if it were a piece of cheese. All of a sudden, the voice, surely reenergized from its brief silence, rings out once more to extol the extraordinary qualities of a cleaning product, only to be interrupted by an opera choir comprising several hundred people, their throats beginning to convulsively spout out the same word sung over two alternating notes, the already hysterical group reaching even more frenzied heights as they set about steamrolling everything in their path. Will the store, swept into this sinkhole of sound, collapse amid the philharmonic torrent? The realities are running a fever of 39 Celsius, lose one moment of weight, but shortly recover a new density.

The voice, meanwhile, reclaims its assertiveness for good.

"Yes, ladies and gentlemen, there is no fee to enter. The spectacle is free of charge. As for our products, they'll help you to save. Buying is the only way to get richer. Your gold risks devaluing, but our prices can only go up. Seize the opportunity, and tell your friends too. Enter our largest bill contest: you could win a fabulous ashtray emblazoned with our monogram and logo: *sic itur ad astra*. Our margarine is renowned. Feed some to your infants, they'll love it for sure. Zero fat guaranteed, and it doesn't stain. Whether you're seeking a personality makeover or to personalize your shopping experience, look no further than our introductory offers. And don't forget that if one of our products has poisoned you, we'll replace it within the hour and cover the burial costs without objection. Have you visited our family menagerie department? Check it out, you won't regret it. Do you have cats at home? Buy them some rats. *À bon chat, bon rat*.[4] But one good dog is worth two small rats in the bush.[5] I'm asking for one minute, just one minute, of your time, as this concerns everyone: Passengers to the impossible, please board on the invisible platform to the right for the first mysterious departure of the day."

There's a large, purplish explosion, and the ceiling shatters into thousands of multicolored tickets that morph into raindrops before reaching the floor. A siren begins wailing and, rising up from a secret garage cleverly concealed beneath the beauty salon, a flaming hot rod peels out in a shower of sparks, spins around, and scorches the floor as its steel arms snatch up shoppers and shove them into the car. The vehicle lifts off from the ground and tilts back, tossing out half the passengers, then traces a portrait of the sales manager's features with its graceful flight path before disappearing into a giant mirrored wardrobe which is immediately swallowed up by the ceiling. Peremptorily, the loudspeaker announces ten nonserious fatalities and one unscathed passenger, who receives the daily surprise deal. In other news, management is pleased to announce that starting now on a trial basis, every bottle of condensed milk purchased will come with two children, and that well-worn thousand-franc bills can be exchanged for brand-new 20-franc pieces, along with a warranty.

Next to me, a woman with three chins is eating a pie for three people, then a Chinese hat adorned with nests of swallows, none of which makes a summer.[6] Farther away, a vacuum cleaner attempts in vain to spit up the protester it has just swallowed; a general in civilian clothes slides a coin into an automatic device and comes to in a drawer.

"Man—and we are certainly proud to affirm it—is advertising's noblest conquest. Rest assured: Razveet kills slowly. Are you in a rush? Why not install a subway in your apartment? We apologize, Madame, for having cut your hand into such thin slices, but it does in fact demonstrate the efficacy of our patented device. A reminder to our wonderful clientele that it's forbidden to let your feral servants run around without a bell collar. And naturally, we've thought of everything. These collars are for sale on the fourth floor.

And this fourth floor is itself on sale on the sixth floor. Compare our prices and you won't hesitate."

Without warning, a secret agent has just started to beat a woman who appeared to hesitate after comparing prices. By contrast, another shopper charges past every obstacle and plows, head down, toward the product in question, sweeping away everything in her path.

"On every floor, our pleasure-to-serve-yous and never-before-seen sales displays await. Check out our slippery-soled slippers, our combustible water heaters, our wallpaper depicting scenes of phosphorescent terror—with an accompanying soundtrack to play after midnight (also available for children)—our travel shrouds, our 'Atocomic' firecracker napkins that will blow up your parents in the middle of their joyous holiday revels. For your own reveille, try our alarms, made by our clockmaker department, then head directly over to the spirituality stand, where you'll find our bathrooms with consecrated hot and cold water, our haloed fruit dishes, our kitchen confessional booths, and the famous 'Our Father' devotional candles that only melt down if you squeeze them."

A vulture glides toward the ground, dives at a child, carries him up to the ceiling, then releases him in a parachute, after which he descends, much aged, in the guise of our legal department head. In the department of Little Trifles, a saleswoman makes a tactless joke about this episode: predictably, she falls into the water; someone volunteering to fish her out falls in himself and perishes of congestion. Inspired by this example, the head of accounting climbs to the top floor, spies a fishbowl in the lobby, dives, misses the bowl by a few centimeters, and crashes into a trombone. A movie director, who happens to have filmed the scene, rewinds it so that the diver finds himself back from where he leapt. He dives again, this time landing in the bowl, and accidentally swallows the two goldfish swimming inside, then dies of shock upon seeing his corpse in the trombone. Come now, Madame, how do you expect to wear a watch when you don't have a wrist on that arm? At the perfume counter, they're calling for volunteers to offer up their throats to test the efficacy of a new brand of razor. Appearing on television, the Pope takes the opportunity to bless the blunt instruments aisle, excommunicate fur sofas, sanctify the four-piece swimsuit adorned with saleswomen, and endorse form-fitting dresses, then spits into the microphone in a saintly manner and blows his nose in conclusion. Some workers try to carry off the store's first level without bumping into the other floors.

"Yes, Monsieur, if you'd like to purify yourself and remain unsullied from the world, try the bain–Mother Mary or the stain-removing Pitcher."

A cloud of green and red flies is suddenly let loose in the store.

"Millions of mosquitos approve of Fly-Tox. What's holding you back? If you're bored by life, treat yourself to a plane ride: you'll never return! Our tombstone display is open on the sixth floor. And our stratospheric balloons for children are for sale on the lower ground floor. Pandering sultans, wear soutanes, they'll sustain your morale."

Mounted atop a white horse, a manager rides from department to department, firing shots from his revolver whenever some detail displeases him, his horse whinnying with delight upon viewing the gross receipts. Stopped short in beatific wonder before a slot machine, an exemplary priest insists on saying mass in the section of special products for unmarried people of both sexes, and a saleswoman hastens to phone the Cardinal in order to avoid a scandal. Furthermore, the slot machine is already launching a rocket whose explosion spews forth a bundle of letters affirming that God created Coca-Cola on the eighth day. The orchestra starts to play the hallelujah hymn, while virgins dressed as soda bottles announce that He has finally been born, the Holy Child. A thousand voices all recommend that curious shoppers head to the second floor, where they are greeted by a giant funnel dispensing jets of Coca-Cola down their throats by force, then directing skeptics to the antiseptic aisle and believers to the prefabricated chapel where pasteurized popes mass-baptize promotional newborns with soda. Farther on, in order to compensate and reassure the true believers, a series of crucifixions are carried out without respite in the nails and home improvement section to demonstrate the various qualities of an indestructible material. A giant cotton snowflake escapes from the first aid station, drifts up, and unleashes a torrent of rain. Cough drops fall from the sky, as well as galoshes and umbrellas, hanging from which are various goodie bags.

"Attention! Try to grab one of these bags. The nonexploding ones have some splendid gifts inside. Try your luck. And don't forget that the best way to win the lottery is still to resell the tickets to your friends. Lost all your friends? Hurry down to the second floor. We've just received a shipment of high-quality ones, guaranteed for one month, and, at no extra cost, you'll receive an assortment of little gifts for the meeting."

A product demonstrator displays his arm that has been roasted in a gas oven, places it on a plate, pours some Madeira wine sauce over it, garnishes it with peas, and offers forks to the foodies in the crowd. Just then, the stand catches fire, but a saleswoman proves that nothing beats a dousing of kerosene for putting out a burgeoning flame. The boss himself descends from above to canonize her, marches the fourth regiment into the store, orders a twelve-volley salute, pins a medal on her, and observes that the shells have damaged a section of the building. Without hesitating, he decides to transform this crater into a swimming pool for customers, who slide seamlessly from the solid floor into the still frigid water. Management deems it opportune to build a tearoom with a terrace ten meters above the disaster zone. One of the platforms collapses, furnishing the survivors with a view of a double catastrophe. Management takes advantage of the accident by doubling its food prices. Accounting teams roam the store calculating profits, the firm buys the neighboring housing blocks, tears down the walls, and forcefully integrates the apartments into the store, a tide of products pours into the dwellings, smothering everyone who can't flee in time. The survivors are conscripted as forced customers, fireworks commemorate the event, pigeons are released, the fireworks singe the pigeons, who fall back to the ground, roasted, onto silver plates, and life goes on.

On the ground floor, just the same as several levels up, life chases its tail, like that glamorous woman scurrying from the register to the wrapping counters. Ditto for the department head who is paid to observe the customers' movements, the stranger who's been following the woman for hours, the store detective following the stranger without suspecting that he's been followed all morning by his wife, herself followed by her lover, along with the lover's wife, as well as her pederast friend, who himself is being tailed by a sister tasked with keeping an eye on his behavior, herself shadowed by a mother who is in turn followed by a relative, not to mention the children who should be following their fathers, children who, by the by, are tailed by the store detective, and the dance begins again in reverse, the whole sequence having so many moving parts that it's no longer possible to determine how it originally started.

"Pontiac time is yours for the taking, gentlemen. You'll never be late to a meeting again; perfectly out of sync, the Pontiac watch constantly adapts to your schedule. If you have nothing left in your wallets, why not leave? The exit, ladies and gentlemen, is free with any purchase over 3,000 francs. Think it over."

Believing that he has reached the exit door, a customer smashes into a mirror. The two figures violently collide, and the man collapses onto the floor as the reflection steps out of the mirror and over the body. A malfunctioning aeration pipe abruptly belches out an enormous puff of customers, the loudspeaker bursts out in laughter as it announces that this very laugh can be found on page 212 of the store catalog and is currently available for purchase; a giant hole puncher breaks free and pierces everything it can sink its teeth into; a retired infantry lieutenant, his horoscope having informed him that staircases will spell trouble, desperately hurls himself into an elevator cage; gloves in a display case pick up and distance themselves from the remaining stock, while thousands of slippers set out, like an army of termites, to attack the mechanical clocks.

Meanwhile, the store's background music is now just a confused bellowing. The loudspeaker isn't hawking any more products but emitting blaring siren sounds. Pouring forth from its mouth are shapeless objects that float for a moment and then break apart in the air, releasing clouds of soot or flour. Saleswomen hand out signed photographs of themselves, others put themselves up for auction, while a few grope any customer within arm's reach. In the heat of the moment, one of them swallows a coin purse, and a running tally flashes in her eyes, while her skull rings with a crystalline jingling. The customers resist her charms as best they can. Private investigators examine their papers, tear up those with blurry fingerprints, and round up anyone whose name has more than two syllables. At the exit, a doorman ushers out the survivors with baton blows. Trucks and tanker cars steer into the lobby to empty their loads. An advertising campaign zestfully announces that all the beds in the furniture department can be rented by the hour for a promotional session with the naked saleswoman of your choice. A television star steps out of the screen to slap his wife, a klutz knocks over several earthenware vases, but the saleswoman has the last word by smashing the vase-smasher with a hammer. An enthusiastic crowd cheers on six old handicapped men racing their wheelchairs in the sports department, while on the stairs, a chair caner stuffs the recovered corpses with straw. A team of workers shows up at the wrong worksite and starts to build a rental property right in the middle of the store. Overwhelmed by the commotion, the saleswomen end up selling their own undergarments, customers step in to take their place, the salesmen become customers, and the head of the company joins up with a group of masons to mix cement, all while giving them instructions in fact meant for the accounting department. Six holy virgins descend from the sky and ask the public to select the lone veridical and officially canonized one among them. Calls to rape and pillage ring out, slips fly above the cafe's windmills, trapdoors open like ice holes, steel objects belch out flashbacklashes, and anodyne questions mutate into bursts of machine-gun fire. The illuminated sign at the undertaker's winks coyly at the funeral hobbyists and greets customers with a malice-filled smile. The head of accounting, who has entered the wrong door while searching for his voice, pins his personality to the wall reserved for advertisements. A monstrous calf emerges from a bottle of condensed milk. People try and fail to tear a socialite away from the profound emotion overcoming her, and a bike officer grazes on the flowers in the upholstery. Journalists take snapshots here and there, the flashes transforming the photographs into literary clichés, while the progressive federation of architect-spies unveils an exhibition of "revolutionary" staircases with two interlacing spirals. Plumbers replace telephone wires with kilometers of coils. Bloody tracks appear all over the store, shadows abruptly dissolve, and, following the debauched logic of the place, the wool section suddenly explodes into the neighboring aisles. Everything becomes woven, wool glass silently shatters from the woolen nuts and bolts raining down, and a woolen plane takes off amid a chorus of panicked sheep. Rats scurry from a counter that sinks like a stone a minute later; a murderous gueridon lays all its crimes on the table, fabric stiffens, gestures emit contagious radiation, wedding cake tiers divorce each another, and the crowd grows rowdy. Aerating mouths gobble up words to relay them to the faucets, which spew them back out in the form of counterfeit banknotes; hands wander in search of their owners, spurts of color emerge from their dens, chemical formulas decompose, atoms revolt against their molecules, outlines fade in the air, and life and death now compose one unbroken network, just as water and fire, light and sound, coalesce into one vague glimmer—when suddenly the store is submerged in total darkness.

And silence.

A projector turns on, and its pale ray fixes on an acrobat hanging in the void, suspended, it appears, by the sole beam of light. He swings, spins around on an invisible trapeze, straightens out, and disappears along with the ray of light.

The daylight returns.

I can no longer see anything but a heap of items smashed together, shapeless, as if washed out by the moisture.

My focus must have shifted, that's it. Because right then, another sight comes into view: behind a wrapping station, there's an employee. He has just snipped the string of a package, then stopped working. He stares into space. He stands there, hands empty, motionless.

I recognize him.

The wrapper, c'est moi.

THE WRAPPER STRAIGHTENS UP and takes a deep breath. Then, without warning, another face seems to slide over his own. That of a man who, while appearing perfectly unscathed, was actually suffering from ravaged intestines.

Finally, he starts to scream.

And everything remains suspended in the wake of that scream of a creature who has just fallen into himself, collapsing in a heap with the certainty that he'll never have the strength to rise back to the surface. I feel the moment of general paralysis that the spine-chilling scream produces throughout the store's six floors.

Then came the laugh, even more terrifying than the scream. For a moment, the man deliberated among several possible acts of aggression. Suddenly, he made his choice: he began to wrap.

But he was no longer the one performing the action. That man disappeared when the scream ceased. And some frenzied thing replaced the wrapper, something with the coiled energy of a wildcat, with gestures marked by an inhuman precision, the driving force of a possessed robot.

He began to wrap as if he were a turbine designed to manipulate two weightless hands, hands of glass and steel, enhanced with the latest technology, finally capable of executing the perfect gesture. The movements were performed so speedily that they blurred together into a single motion. It was impossible to isolate the moment in which he picked up the scissors or the wrapping paper, impossible to dissect his action. Working at speeds surpassing the speed of light, he tore off a sheet of paper, laid it out flat, wrapped the package, stuck on the label, tied it up, tossed it aside, and took another sheet, every completed package as impeccably wrapped as if dozens of specialists had thought through and worked on the task for hours.

He started to wrap everything within reach. You name it, he wrapped it. Products from the neighboring department, chairs and shipping cartons, tools and cash drawers, the personal items of customers and the shoes of saleswomen. Everything, and as soon as you could make out what he was wrapping, as soon as some shape was deposited onto the table, it was replaced by another that disappeared as well, wrapped up in a miraculously tailored straitjacket, made to measure, tied up, and just as soon tossed aside. Then he descended into parody. Working faster yet, he began to caricaturize himself, pantomiming delirium, transfiguring everything, shredding his motions with such spectacular virtuosity that each movement seemed to spew forth flakes and sparks, confetti and crystal balls. Switching from juggling to acrobatics, he perched himself on the table and started to wrap objects floating in thin air four feet above the flat surface, manipulating the laws of geometry in three dimensions with the unadulterated madness of a raving lunatic. Without pausing, he started to deliver a monologue, ranging in register from treble to bass, parodying hundreds of dissimilar voices, incorporating pell-mell the text from posters, advertising slogans, customers' questions and replies, reproaches and static, laughter and screams, conversations and the thousands of syllables ceaselessly sputtering throughout this enormous covered market.

Then, stopping neither his wrapping nor his monologue, balancing yet more pyramids on top of his pyramid-stacking routine, he dreamt up other roles to perform, every observable type in this place, of the customer and the store detective, the saleswoman and the cashier, imitating some, imagining others, switching from one to another without segues, putting on an uninterrupted display of virtuosity with no respite nor any sign of fatigue. And wrapping all the while.

Then, when he had nothing left to wrap, he stepped away from the table, seized a saleswoman, fashioned her a well-fitting cloche hat from the paper, tossed the parcel on the table, tried and failed to flatten her curves underneath the wrapping, smoothed out all the creases, took the ball of string . . .

"Need I point out that you're fired?" says a voice.

What could I say to that?

I exit the mall lobby, and the elevator takes me to the top floor, where I find myself in a completely bare hallway save for the frames of several handleless doors.

I pushed one of them open at random. It opens onto two rooms at once, each unfurnished, peeling paint on the walls. No windows and sky-high ceilings. Empty rooms, and yet Mygale lives here. There she is, dressed in black like a blob of tar.

She looks at me, but just barely and without any feeling, like some indeterminate thing. Her mouth is straight, drawn, taut. Her features are as clearly defined as ever, frozen in an expression of refusal.

"There's nothing to eat," Mygale says. "I didn't go out this month."

Her voice matches her face, tuneless and numb.

"Are you sick?"

She shakes her head very slowly, as if to express the depths of her regret at never being ill.

"Do you have any money left?" I ask her next.

"No, nothing left."

"How do you get by?"

"Beats me. I don't do anything.

"It's Christmas," she adds after a brief pause.

Oh, really? What's there to do?

"Do you need anything?"

"I can't think of anything," she says.

"Goodbye," I tell her.

"Yes, goodbye."

Beneath the glacial chill of our words, I seem to detect the powerful drumbeat of "possiblys" that will never come to pass. Something is required, yes. We realize it. But what action should we take? Would things really improve if I suddenly hammered a nail in the wall? Just like that, for no reason. But where to find a hammer, or a nail? Not to mention the will to raise the hammer?

I leave.

It was almost nighttime that day. However, it was still early, a beautiful morning night without an afternoon and a low-hanging sky hovering just several meters above the rooftops and hemmed in by two zones of dropless rain. Cathedrals and large monuments rose above this sky ceiling, their upper reaches shielded from view.

The entire city resembled a powerful blind mouth, spread open in an obscenely wide, rancorous yawn, and each building stood like a tooth ready to bite, as silently as a smooth-running grinder.

One could sense that people had lost the will to fight. Almost everyone had taken shelter behind the facades of buildings. Several stragglers hugged the walls in rags and slippers, their faces covered with veils, mimicking the demeanor of those condemned to death. You could have sworn it was going to rain soot. The heat dried out one's lips, felt reptilian. A municipal official marked all the odd-numbered doors with a cross in black paint. An abandoned worker emerged from a manhole, a human skull perched atop an athlete's body. Traps had been laid all over the place. Scattered across the sidewalks, Death's delegates strode here and there, and sometimes pedestrians would ask them for a light without realizing the danger they were in.

A doorman in an especially dark side street waved me over.

"Come on in," he told me.

The building he welcomed me into was built of red bricks, and every square inch was dripping with grime, as if the squalid interior had oozed into the facade. But it was in fact just that, a facade, as at the end of a grubby hallway I discovered a door leading to an elegant movie house. I went in and found myself in the alleyway I'd just left. The doorman was there.

"Come on in," he told me.

I walked down the grimy hallway. I found the door again, the same one, because there were no others, but this time, the door led to a wide hall flowing into a number of unfurnished, somber, wood-paneled rooms. The setup was reminiscent of a trading floor. Hundreds of men were working in this labyrinth.

"Everyone's here but you," a stranger comes up to me and declares.

"By the time I got here," I tell him, "here I am."

"Very well. Get to work."

There's important business to conduct. Some discuss matters among themselves, while others walk from room to room, preoccupied. Everyone's hands are always empty, however. It's plain to see that no one here needs any implements. This is commerce in its pure state, with no objective, no concern for profits and losses, no budgets. And all the professions are represented. The utmost solemnity is de rigueur. An assistant, hands in his pocket, offers around the stock listings. They spend, offer, value, sell. They ask to speak to people on the phone, and those people then disappear without a trace. Some of them engage in veritable chess matches in which they constantly vary and reformulate their tactics. Depending on the conversational flow, a stockbroker can transform into a tramp or an accountant, a safety inspector or street sweeper; a concierge one moment and now a financier, just as he will become a shipping magnate or sales rep several minutes hence.

And yet, there are still laws and regulations to be respected. In fact, a bailiff approaches me and asks for my papers. I show them to him.

"Are you a member of the Circle?" he asks.

I'm back out on the street. I'm obviously not getting anywhere and have nothing to do. Perhaps it's time to register with the nearest unemployment office.

They receive me very courteously.

"Do you swear on the Holy Bank to renounce working until your death?"

"I swear it."

"On your honor, do you agree to insult plowmen, industry workers, and the industrious?"

I agree and am handed a card.

But my name is expunged the next day: I was seen raising my glass to the inventor of hourly leaves for strikers.

"You start by raising a glass, and you end up smack in the middle of the marketplace," the official in charge of revoking cards tells me.

Leaving this planet is now my sole desire. But where should I go? I abandon myself to fate.

It chooses Logaros S.

MY VISITS TO LOGAROS S. are always tinged with a bit of melancholy. This planet actually figures in my childhood memories. My parents would regularly send me here to rest. This practice was always roundly criticized, as no one ever believed in this world concealed deep within the star charts.

Logaros S., I must admit, has no striking features, with the exception of one particularity: there's no landscape. The planet is just one flat surface, smooth and transparent and irreproachably tidy, so much so that it almost seems like a surface without matter, a void stretched out lengthwise. Moreover, there is no climate. It's always pleasant, it never rains, and no breezes ever kick up. By contrast, the light changes color every four hours. It can be blue, then red or green or yellow. Never black.

There are no traces of mineral, vegetal, or animal life anywhere. Only the void germinates. It's perfect for resting, and the only possible activity is walking. I leisurely cover kilometers, stopping occasionally to admire not the view but rather that there never is one.

Before heading back to Earth, I decide to visit some worlds which I've already seen but am always happy to revisit. I've always had a passion for rambling.

I see them all again. The moles of Synphes that have for centuries tried to discover a lost civilization; the Grèses, a lower order of sponges nestled within a giant sponge in space; the Noctarnes, who feed on their own fat; the Jogolees, who are in a centuries-long battle with the color orange; the Fyctes, who are nothing more than the symbols and numbers of a gigantic equation; the Stalpes and the Calendres, the Drugues and the Argogyres, the adipose tissues and the larvae, the incandescents and the mineralized, the groundcovers and the madragènes, the tracéphales, the supervertebrates, and the troglophènes. Though these aliens are not human, they're just as disappointing. Like us, they have their trivial problems, and like us, they wake each morning perpetually condemned to dread the prospect of another day identical to the last.

I encounter them all once more, yes, all of them, the tamed and those lacking eyes to see me, those who figure in my childhood memories or who populate my future dreams, as well as those who, for one reason or another, are pinned to the backdrop of my life.

Occasionally along my haphazard flight, I come across one of my acquaintances or a distant relative in some forgotten world. On Acaria-Extinct, I furtively spy a young version of my mother trying to find her way in the world. On Algae-Death, I revisit the demented civilization that sprang from a book of crossword puzzles I left there ten years prior and which the inhabitants have been interpreting according to their own whims. On Ifrage, death currently reigns supreme because of the mirrors brought in by foreign traders in exchange for the planet's ore. On Agavis 45, I recognize the branch of a business I used to work for back on Earth, as well as the boss, who pretends to know who I am and claims that I should have given him a month's notice. An even more unpleasant surprise awaits me farther on in Damle-the-Illusory: a bill for my last month's rent. Finally, on Scyge, I am accused of committing an act of public indecency on Alfagore seven years earlier. All this puts me in a reflective mood. Am I destined to end up in some wasteland standing before the tombstone waiting for me on Earth? Anyway, I check the time: it's already December. I should start thinking about heading back.

Without worrying too much about collisions, always a possibility, I revel in flying low over my past. At the speed of light, you see only a gray, dense mass, an enormous piece of stale bread. I gain altitude, maneuver like a shark, pass by the planet Stragosque, which is riddled through with innumerable tunnels, then descend straight into a succession of apotheoses and jets of fire. Loopy from these acrobatics, I get lost in the Milky Way, and then, after flying by a meteor, I let myself fall like a dead leaf into a winter I can't manage to place. Resolving to take a shortcut home, I attempt to cut through the future, whose guileful melody I can already hear, but I run into a tornado spinning in the opposite direction and, carried away in its drift, end up instead in an abyss of bygone centuries. This chasm is particularly deep, filling my lungs with its shadows. It's a great relief when I reach the gleaming rays of one of the four small suns in the Purple Galaxy. I descend in a tailspin, barely faster than a falling snowflake, narrowly miss getting crushed by a nearly invisible planet that I hadn't spotted, then gain altitude and speed to charge through a six-year-long world war, the entirety of which I experience as an explosion lasting just one second.

Unable to see or hear anything, I cling to my controls. My head's spinning, and my stomach's in knots. I've allowed myself to descend from too high, and I no longer know who I am. This loss of consciousness is dangerous. I must at the very least recall my date of birth and know when I'm scheduled to die; landings are fatal for those who don't respect traffic laws. Luckily, I manage to calm down a bit, gather myself, and assess the situation. I look at my instrument panel. Just 76 million kilometers to go and I'll be home. While I'm at it, I should probably be asking myself where I am. Not me . . . I ask where I'm going to end up. In which job, which role, which year?

I'm mulling over these questions when a jolt surprises me. There's a clicking sound, and then another jolt. Something is definitely happening. My speed is holding steady, the altitude too, but the time needle is oscillating as if malfunctioning. The hours and minutes needles are fixed on zero, with the hour hand quivering. I must have committed some blunder.

I'm still surrounded by darkness and silence, but objects are already whizzing by me, like ribbons carried aloft up by some abstract tornado. There are glimmers of light and splotches of color, forms without definition or crosshatchings desperately trying to attach themselves to a reality.

And here I am sucked up, carried along between two tidal waves. If I listen closely, I can hear the flow of time, like a blast of toxic gas. There are many hazards. First and foremost, running aground in the sands of dead time periods. Or getting trapped in the murderous whirlpool of its verb tense agreements. As if on cue, a massive time span rises up just then, resplendent, and I narrowly avoid it.

I try to regain my equilibrium and change course to outer space, but in vain. I'm still falling, and the hours pass by, minutes rain then spill over into seconds, unleashing a torrent. Waves of hours course through a spring morning, which suddenly crumples into a stormy night that soon disintegrates into an indefinite duration. An entire epoch swirls around itself, then, growing dizzy, drifts away and collapses into a conjugation of the imperfect tense. A moment of respite lets me glimpse the vision of lost time suspended between life and death. The dust of ages clouds my eyes, and I find it difficult to catch my breath. But time is spilling out of me as my blood eventually will. I summon all my willpower to stop this hemorrhaging. The needle jumps from one century to another, lurching in nervous tics. Years fly by like shadows, the months fall like leaves, minutes rise again to the surface, and months of anticipation are drowned under forgotten moments. An icy wind sweeps up a bloody day that dissolves after having catapulted an anachronism. Hundreds of conjugations deviate from their path, pulverizing the conditionals of a still very distant future. Intervals succumb to the dizziness they've just intensified, and nights fling themselves into mirages of the following day. A dead season crawls in search of the tomb of future centuries. A season snaps shut with the brutality of a jawbone, time ends up scheduling itself and weaves extensions whose filaments scour my vision. An eventuality of unbearable brilliance knocks me over. I brace myself, distraught, lashed, blinded. I close my eyes and can no longer see anything. A jolt more violent than the others indicates I'm in a freefall. I try one last time to pull myself together. I look at the dial. The needle has stopped on a date.

1920.

I murmur this date to myself. It's over: I hadn't yet been born in 1920. This is the end, but also not, as the needle trembles and moves to 1934, changes direction again, hesitant, a little tipsy one might say, then goes limp, almost liquified. 1934, 1935, 1927, 1968. It rises, it falls, it rises again, falls back down, and down further and further. Colors and spots, shadows and flashes burst into view. Visions, most often hazy, appear before me from time to time, speeding by like race cars in a massive asphalt pipe.

Doors slam behind retreating air currents, and liquid rushes into objects without any definable contours. Rags become rain clouds and hills try to rise up, the entire sky is seized by a secret law of gravity and collapses in a squeaking of foam. Invisible windows shatter, tentacles ribbed with human nerves attempt to escape from imaginary dangers, outlines distend like rubber bands. Everywhere, shapes are baring their claws, escape routes open up across pale, shifting ground, while luck confronts sound, undertaking a series of shrewd maneuvers before voraciously devouring itself. Theorems without numbers or proofs collapse under their own gratuitousness, lost mishaps burrow into the night like moles, and as the maturity date rears up from the depths of its forfeiture, a coincidence fails to materialize, then staggers and gets bogged down in an uproar without a cause.

And still the same frenetic dial . . . 1929 . . . 1957 . . . 1932 . . . a sudden leap forward, 1944 . . . nosedive . . . 1923, I'm born—finally born—I'll be able to die . . . 1937, I grow up . . . 1930 . . . I shrink. 1968 . . . 1969 . . . 1939 . . . 1998, I surpass the time barrier, the life barrier, the death barrier, the final barrier, and then the final barrier of the true ending beyond the ultimate negation of time past, present, and future . . .

Objects continue to stream by rapidly, straining the bounds of perception. I can now sense their personal connection to me. I must have reentered my own life without realizing it. I burst into it, am scattered across my allotted duration here. I exist as flames lasting less than one-tenth of a second. I'm nothing more than an explosion, a flash, a multiplicity. I'm ablaze, I scorch myself, and yet still feel alive.

1935, here I am as a salesman, then as a reseller—resold, reclaimed, returned, redeparted, repurchased, liquidated . . . 1939, a corporate director flings a bunch of envelopes in my face, sends me off, and I leave with the entire building, the entire neighborhood, trailing behind me . . . 1943, I fall, I fall lower and lower, becoming a novelist, then a literary critic . . . 1925, it's hot this winter, the town is now just a vast swamp of treacly water in which I try to locate my submerged family . . . 1935, I've been traveling for months, checked like luggage, from baggage locker to locker, station to station, until I finally clear customs and . . . 1960, I'm hungry, thirsty, tired, and yet I've attained the height of fame and riches. I'm so respected, in fact, that no one dares accept my money . . . 1989, nothing, I see nothing, this rude ascent has clouded my vision . . . 1946, I've forgotten my name, I've lost my "large family" card and wander through the streets begging for a provisional identity, when they scoop me up, slap me with a bill, and file me with the legislature . . . 1945, the year's completely empty: the molecules are on strike . . . 1950, what a hungry year . . . 1944, it's so dark . . . 1955, help! Help! But what's the matter? . . . 1956, "I'm sorry," says a voice to me; then another, then thousands of others . . . 1937, who, then, has the audacity to laugh as I'm about to speak, and why does this laugh abruptly shatter a year that had started out so well? . . . 1962, I no longer have arms, a rope alone binds me to life, and I drag a barge loaded with rocks of no use to anyone along an endless canal . . . 1924, my apartment is a giant spider's web in which objects watch every move I make through their enormous, phosphorescent eyes, always immobile, lying in wait . . . 1931, I visit a cemetery, it's raining, I sink into the mud along with a pot of chrysanthemums, I disappear, I'm now a mere flowerpot at the grave of an unknown person, who smiles at me from within his mother-of-pearl locket . . . 1945, smudges, shapes, a confusion with a vile stench . . . 1987, the larvae of things vainly trying to hatch . . . 1967, a filament, a spark, then nothing

. . . 1928, still nothing . . . 1952, nothing either . . . the needle is currently jumping from one number to another so rapidly that I can no longer keep up. It's nothing but a blur of steel at this point. It's no longer any specific time. I'm no longer anywhere. There's no longer anything. I'm alone, lost in the depths of nothingness. I must have risen too high or fallen too far. I have to know which, must know this above all else. The telephone. How did I not think of it sooner? I can still sort everything out.

"Hello, hello . . . Listen to me carefully. I'm falling. I'm in danger of living or dying. What time is it? Do you hear me? What time is it? It's a matter of life or death."

No one responds. I expected as much. I must have shot past the date of my death and that of my birth. Or I also might have foundered in an intermediary dimension, a dead-end street perhaps. It's all over. Finally, I have nothing left to fear. Everything is possible from here on out.

The time is precisely 0 o'clock, 0 minutes, and 1/1000 of a second. It's neither day nor night. There's no temperature. I'm falling, but I'm free from danger, as no ground will ever claim me. I sink, I drown, I fly, I resuscitate, and, submerged in this temporal wave, start laughing before I'm spit back to the surface coughing, then refashion myself, rewrite myself, liquify myself, efface myself. Finally, I can give birth to my mother, wipe out a century's worth of history by snapping my fingers, order the clocks to call every second to arms, ring the bell, and start marching backward to the creation of the world. On my orders . . . Attention! Let the universe be, and it was. I bequeath to it the square wheel and ultra-dry water, I invent high-fidelity silence, literary gas, fireless smoke, the edgeless hole, and the year without night—I try in vain to surprise myself.

I'm any old thing, no longer anything. I will never be anything. It could be raining, lightning could strike me, the wind could cut me in two, and I'd be neither soaked nor fried nor halved. Why is it so cold in me? A summer, that's what I need. Do you hear? I order you to deliver a scorching July month with a late-afternoon storm of rage and despair.[7] It's all about knowing what one wants. Now, I can move forward. Everything around me is boggy, foggy, groggy, soggy. How wonderful not to live.

To amuse myself, I lay: waste to a day, siege to a decommissioned sky, a feeling to rest, and bare five hypotheses after making them justify themselves. I toss an unexpected outcome well past the reach of a lawyerless case and then, spying a suspicion, squash it. Logic seeks to intervene: instantly squaring it, I transform it into a vicious circle. As I'm breaking through to the fourth dimension, an explosion of salguese holifies me and accipitates while derosating a soptic of aramides. And yet, I keep on falling. I know it, I can feel it.

From where? To where? Through what? Unanswered questions. I fall completely through to the other side of my own descent. Finally, a chance to verify whether there is another void behind that of the twenty-four hours we so zealously try to fill. But the fall is so long, so slow. What is up and what is down? Left or right? Past or future? It's now or never, the time to reflect on this past, to rip out the entire score and feed it into the delirious mechanism of the thousand-keyed player piano I can salvage from any wreckage whatsoever. It's now or never to let ultrasounds rain down over human affairs and toss formless memories into this tumult, scraps of unlived lives, snippets of futures impossible to realize. Juggling quicker, always quicker, borrowing several hands to assist the effort, but never letting the tempo slow, adding in several trumpet blasts, a failed dream, a half-refusal, a zesting of fear. Mix well. Season with a soupçon of regret. Don't let it cool. And please, as quickly as possible, sprinkle with ten grams of nitroglycerine, pour over a liter of hemlock, two drops of glue here, a little mending job there, move faster under pain of death, faster than speed itself, so fast as to finally bridge life and death, to pass from one month to another skipping over several unimportant years and taking advantage of this frictionless freefall to smile at the goal, smile at whatever, without cause or reason, without a face and without features, to smile without smiling and without any desire to do so . . .

But it's too late: that old certitude overtakes me. At the same time, I feel a migraine coming on. That's a bad sign: I'm approaching the realities. They'll show up any minute. Where will I land, then? In my past? In the past of a stranger? At what date? And in what form? As an animal with flower petals? Or as some mangled thing torn to shreds by the darkness, flattened by the pressure I've endured, unknown, anonymous, unidentifiable?

I'm certain of one thing: I've arrived. There's ground beneath my feet and a roof over my head. A gray floor. A gray ceiling. Those of a hallway, it would seem.

A clock shows 10:06, a calendar 12 April. How about that, it's my birthday tomorrow.

There's a door in front of me.

Naturally, I open it.

Naturally, he's behind it:

"Ah, is that you, Sternberg? Late again, naturally. I did warn you that you *absolutely* needed to be on time today. What goes through that head of yours . . ."

TRANSLATOR'S NOTES

1. A garbled combination of the metro station Sèvres-Babylone and the quai de Denfert-Rochereau.
2. Postes, Telégraphes, Téléphones: a since disbanded government department.
3. The original French is *faute de frère, on mangera du cerf-volant*, a nonsense version of the proverb *faute de grives, on mange des merles*, meaning "Make do with what you have," "Beggars can't be choosers," etc.
4. *À bon chat, bon rat* (literally "To a good cat, a good rat"): a French expression roughly meaning "Two can play at that game."
5. Playing on a Boris Vian line: *Un bon chien vaut mieux que deux kilos de rats*, "A good dog is worth more than two kilos of rats."
6. Referring to the expression *Une hirondelle ne fait pas le printemps*, or "One swallow does not a summer make."
7. The original French, *orage au désespoir*, echoes a famous line from Don Diègue in Corneille's *Le Cid*: "Ô rage! ô désespoir! ô vieillesse ennemie!"

Matt Seidel has been employed as a French literary agent, graduate teaching assistant, academic editor, transcriber, staff writer for the online literary magazine *The Millions*, contributor to *Publishers Weekly*, and now a translator.